Blaze

Alaska—the last frontier.

*The nights are long. The days are cold.
And the men are really, really HOT!*

Can you think of a better excuse for a trip up north?

*Come on back to the unorthodox and unforgettable
town of Good Riddance and experience some...*

Alaskan Heat!

Watch for:

**NORTHERN FASCINATION
October 2011**

**"NORTHERN FANTASY"
(in Merry Christmas, Baby
a Blazing Christmas anthology)
December 2011**

**NORTHERN FIRES
February 2012**

Enjoy the adventure!

Dear Reader,

I'm so happy to be back in Good Riddance, Alaska, with you. Even though the series only started last year, it seems to have touched a chord with a lot of readers. I'm glad people love the place as much as I do.

Many of my readers asked me to give Jenna Rathburne her own happy ending. And there's nobody more deserving. Jenna's the girl you'd love to hate, but she's just so darn nice, you can't. She possesses the proverbial heart of gold and an ability to see the best in everyone.

Not just any hero would do for Jenna. She deserved a man who would see and appreciate the real woman inside. At first glance, Logan Jeffries, a former high school acquaintance, seems like a long shot when he shows up in Good Riddance. But nothing overcomes obstacles like true love.

If you've been before, I hope you enjoy returning to Good Riddance. If this is your first time, well, I hope you'll come back. I love to hear from readers. You can drop me a line or visit me at www.jenniferlabrecque.com.

Happy reading!

Jennifer LaBrecque

Jennifer LaBrecque

NORTHERN FASCINATION

Harlequin®

TORONTO NEW YORK LONDON
AMSTERDAM PARIS SYDNEY HAMBURG
STOCKHOLM ATHENS TOKYO MILAN MADRID
PRAGUE WARSAW BUDAPEST AUCKLAND

Recycling programs
for this product may
not exist in your area.

ISBN-13: 978-0-373-79646-5

NORTHERN FASCINATION

Copyright © 2011 by Jennifer LaBrecque

This edition published by arrangement with Harlequin Books S.A.

For questions and comments about the quality of this book please contact us at Customer_eCare@Harlequin.ca.

® and TM are trademarks of the publisher. Trademarks indicated with ® are registered in the United States Patent and Trademark Office, the Canadian Trade Marks Office and in other countries.

www.Harlequin.com

Printed in U.S.A.

ABOUT THE AUTHOR

After a varied career path that included barbecue-joint waitress, corporate numbers cruncher and bug-business maven, Jennifer LaBrecque has found her true calling writing contemporary romance. Named 2001 Notable New Author of the Year and 2002 winner of the prestigious Maggie Award for Excellence, she is also a two-time RITA® Award finalist. Jennifer lives in suburban Atlanta with a Chihuahua who runs the whole show.

Books by Jennifer LaBrecque

HARLEQUIN BLAZE
206—DARING IN THE DARK
228—ANTICIPATION
262—HIGHLAND FLING
367—THE BIG HEAT
401—NOBODY DOES IT BETTER
436—YULE BE MINE
465—HOT-WIRED
499—RIPPED!
537—BLAZING BEDTIME STORIES, VOLUME V
        "Goldie and the Three Brothers"
570—NORTHERN EXPOSURE
575—NORTHERN ENCOUNTER
581—NORTHERN ESCAPE
598—IN THE LINE OF FIRE

To get the inside scoop on Harlequin Blaze and its talented writers, be sure to check out blazeauthors.com.

Don't miss any of our special offers. Write to us at the following address for information on our newest releases.

Harlequin Reader Service
U.S.: 3010 Walden Ave., P.O. Box 1325, Buffalo, NY 14269
Canadian: P.O. Box 609, Fort Erie, Ont. L2A 5X3

In memory of Maurice L. Beckett
and the love he shared with Emily Beckett.

Prologue

LOGAN JEFFRIES TRIED TO organize his thoughts around the afternoon's debate in a quarter of an hour. As captain he needed his wits about him. The team had yet to lose a match under his direction, the same as when his father had been debate team captain back in the day. Thus far, he was doing a decent job of "upholding the Jeffries tradition."

However, thought organization was easier said than done when Jenna Rathburne was in the vicinity. He dialed the combination to his locker and opened it. He'd just passed her in the hall. As usual, he'd looked the other way when he walked by. He'd be damned if he'd be the geek caught staring at the prettiest, most popular girl in school, especially since the halls had cleared out considerably since the last bell had sounded half an hour ago.

With his head buried in his locker, he *felt* her before he saw her. It was as if every nerve ending in his body fired off a signal to his brain when she was in his immediate vicinity. Maybe she was waiting for someone who had a locker near his. He straightened but steadfastly stared straight ahead.

She cleared her throat. "Uh…hey, Logan."

Startled she'd actually sought him out, he turned. His heart pounding, his breath stuck somewhere inside him, he managed to respond. "Hi."

"So, are you ready for the debate this afternoon?"

He stood there, clueless. His brain didn't seem to be fully functioning. Thank God she wasn't part of the debate team—as unlikely as him joining the cheer squad—or he'd flub every match for sure. "Yeah. I guess."

Brilliant. Scintillating. He searched for something clever but came up blank. Instead he just stared at her.

Her blond hair was caught up in a ponytail. He'd always known her eyes were blue but up close this way, they were more intense. But then again, everything was more intense—the pounding of his heart, the swing of her hair against her shoulder, the way his stomach knotted in his gut.

She shifted from one foot to another and if he hadn't known better, he might've thought she was as nervous as him. That, however, was highly improbable considering her popularity, her cuteness and the fact she was cheerleading captain.

"I, uh, wanted to ask if you'd escort me to the Homecoming game. You know, unless you already have another date or something." Her words came out in a breathless rush.

Logan stood stock-still for a moment, certain he'd heard her wrong. For a second, he thought she'd just asked him to escort her to one of biggest events in high school. "Huh?"

"If you're available, would you escort me to Homecoming?"

He hadn't heard her wrong. Jenna had just asked him to be her date.

Something over her shoulder caught his attention. Her best friend, Bethany, stood over by the water fountain staring at the two of them. When she caught him looking at her, she quickly turned and drank from the fountain, as if that's why she'd been there all along.

The logic which served him so well as debate captain took over. Okay. Right. Now it all made sense. This had to be some kind of dare. The whole thing was a set-up. He was supposed to say yes and then Jenna and Bethany would collapse into hysterical laughter, as would everyone else once they all heard that Logan Jeffries, who was supposed to be so smart, had been dumb enough to really think Jenna Rathburne wanted to go out with him.

"Thanks but no thanks. Homecoming's not really my deal."

For a split second he thought he saw tears shimmer in her eyes but it must've been the lighting. She pasted on her mega-watt smile. "Sure. Thanks. Okay, have a nice day."

"Yeah, you, too." He turned his attention back to his locker, as if the contents fascinated him.

"Um, good luck today with the debate."

"Thanks."

He saw, out of his peripheral vision, her turn and walk away.

That was one humiliating experience narrowly averted. He'd very nearly made an utter fool of himself.

1

Twelve years later...

JENNA STEPPED OUT ONTO Good Riddance, Alaska's snow-covered sidewalk, into the last of the October sun's dying rays.

Edging back into the middle of Main Street, Norris Watts dodged a pothole and waved Jenna more to the left. "I want to make sure I get the entire window in the shot." Curl's lettered window was something of an attention grabber. Curl's Taxidermy, Barber Shop, Salon and Mortuary.

"Wait. Let me grab Tama. He needs to be in the photo, too."

Norris sighed. "Fine, go get the cat." Norris wasn't really put out. She liked Tama as much as everyone else did.

Jenna dashed back into Curl's and picked up the big Maine Coon mix lounging on top of his scratching post on the far side of the room. "C'mon, you big punkin', photo op."

Tama blinked at her, unimpressed and she laughed, pressing a kiss to his furry head. She'd adopted him two months ago from a no-kill shelter in Anchorage. He was, without a doubt, the most awesome, perfect cat on the planet. Of course, he just happened to be her very first pet ever but he was still perfect.

He went everywhere with Jenna, except Gus's. Honestly, it was as if he was half dog because he followed her everywhere. She adored her fur-baby.

Holding Tama, Jenna stood to the right as Norris had previously directed. "How's this?" She held up one of Tama's paws as if he was waving and said to him, "Say kitty treat."

"Perfect," Norris said, speaking without removing the lit cigarette in her mouth. Her gravelly voice interested Jenna. The older woman, an unapologetic chain smoker, sounded as if she'd been puffing a pack of unfiltered cigarettes a day since birth.

She fired off a couple of shot. "Perfect. We needed to get those shots before the sun was gone completely. Now just a couple more questions, if you don't mind."

"Sure." Jenna didn't mind. She liked Norris. She liked everyone in Good Riddance.

Norris, even more of a newcomer than Jenna, had retired to Good Riddance in June after a forty-something year stint as a reporter for a daily newspaper in Philadelphia. At first content with spending the longer days of the Alaskan summer fishing and camping, Norris had claimed to be bored out of her skull once the days began to shorten. She'd decided Good Riddance and the other remote towns needed a local newspaper to keep folks in touch with what was going on locally.

Because Jenna was one of the newer residents and a business owner, Norris wanted to do a "feature" on her. While Jenna didn't much see herself as particularly newsworthy, she was all for helping a friend. So here they were.

The photo over with, Norris took a final drag off her cigarette and extinguished it. She dropped the butt in a little tin she carried with her.

They stepped back into the "front room" of Curl's where Jenna worked at a table in the small rectangular room. A sink and a barber chair shared the area as well. Compliments of the taxidermy and mortuary located in the rear, a faint odor of formaldehyde always hung in the air, blending with the scent of nail polish and remover.

Luckily, Curl's animal stuffing business was a whole lot more active than his funeral home gig. In the past year there'd only been one funeral. While it had been kind of sad, they lived in a place where life and death seemed more accepted as the natural order of things.

Jenna returned Tama to his platform and gave him the promised kitty treat, earning a head bump against her hand. Crossing the room, she sat in the straight chair behind the table.

"So, I understand you initially came to Good Riddance with your former fiancé, Tad Weatherspoon?" Norris eyed the straight chair on the opposite side of the table and shook her head.

"That's right." *That* had been a close call.

Norris settled in the barber chair and swiveled it around to face Jenna. "But once you got here, you found out he was still married to the town founder and mayor, Merrilee Danville Weatherspoon Swenson?" Norris popped a stick of chewing gum in her mouth. "Sounds kind of like a soap opera to me."

"Yeah, I guess it does. Life's sort of like that sometimes. Except on the soaps, they're always dressed up nice all the time—like that would happen in real life—and there are no commercial breaks."

Lucky, a retired Army cook who had taken over Gus's, the town restaurant, was addicted to two soap operas. From noon until two, Monday through Friday, both televisions in the place were tuned in. He'd even been known to burn a grilled cheese or two if there was a high-drama scene involved. These days, half the town crammed in to watch them, too.

"So, Tad was still married to Merrilee. And nobody in town guessed Merrilee was married, either?"

Norris said, shaking her head. "You've got to love a married man with a fiancée on the side."

"Tell me about it. He said we were just coming for a visit. It turned out the reason for the visit was because he needed Merrilee to sign the divorce papers so he could marry me."

"But you didn't marry him?"

"Hel-lo, Norris. I'm here and he's not."

"I'm just checking facts."

Jenna nodded. "No wedding there. I didn't want to marry a liar. He'd lied about being divorced, his age and who knows what else at that point. I decided he wasn't the kind of man I was meant to be with." She'd mistakenly thought an older man had meant stability. Boy, had she been wrong.

"Why'd you stay here instead of going back to Georgia with him?"

"While I was here, I'd popped into Curl's to check out the place out since he advertised a salon. I have a beauty supply store back in Georgia which is doing well. I've got a great manager and it's set up as a profit-share. Every employee, after being with the company for six months, gets a percentage of the profits. They treat my business like it's their own, because…well, it kind of is. Anyway, Curl and I got to talking and I wound up doing a couple of manicures for free with some nail polish I had in my suitcase." It had been fun and the people were interesting, which was more than she could say about Tad at that stage.

"I discovered I really liked it here. So Tad left and I stayed."

To say she liked it here was an understatement. All she'd ever wanted was some stability in her life and a place where she could put down roots. Her heart had recognized Good Riddance as that place.

Tad had been mad as a wet hen. She smiled, thinking of him clucking instead of strutting around like the rooster he liked to pretend he was. "It was the best move I ever made. Well, actually, I guess you could say being engaged to Tad was the best move I ever made. Otherwise I wouldn't have ever come here. I'd never heard of the place before."

Norris nodded, scribbling furiously on her notepad. "And now, eleven months later, you're building a destination spa."

"It's more like a co-op spa." She was setting it up the same as her other business. She'd found a couple of part-timers couldn't handle all the requests coming her way. She was still looking for someone to cover the massage end. "My nail business has outgrown Curl's and I've had a lot of requests for massages and facials." She'd done a couple of facials in the barber chair but it just wasn't the same. "Just because a woman lives in the wilderness doesn't mean she has to look like she dies. I've got bookings already lined up into the spring."

"And you're scheduled to open the new facility when?"

"Well, the exterior's just being finished up," she said, as if Norris hadn't seen the new building going up every day for the past couple of weeks. "And they'll spend the next month working on the interior. We're scheduled to open the first of December."

Norris knew all of this. Heck, everybody in Good Riddance knew, but what the heck, Jenna would go over it again in an interview format if that's what Norris wanted.

"Just in time for Chrismoose?" Norris said.

Chrismoose was way cool. Jenna was even more excited about it this year because she knew what was coming. There was a lot to be said for anticipation. The whole town had a festival the week before Christmas because some hermit guy named Chris used to ride his pet moose into town every year with toys for the kids. Merrilee had turned it into a tradition after Chris had passed away. People came from all over the area to join in the fun and games.

Jenna nodded, "We're already booked solid for Chrismoose." She'd had to turn business down.

"Tell me one thing about you that no one here knows."

Jenna didn't know how to cook, but really, pretty much everyone knew that. She'd adopted a cat from a rescue shelter six months ago, but who didn't know Tama who was curled up sleeping in the sink now behind the barber's chair? Heck, she brought him to work with her every day.

She was a virgin. If Norris thought the business with Tad, Jenna and Merrilee sounded like a soap opera, she'd really pass out at that admission. Then again, Jenna would probably pass out if that fact got around. It was a conscious choice she'd made. Not necessarily to wait until she got married, but she at least wanted her first time to be special. But she hadn't yet met a guy who tripped her trigger. Back in the day, she'd had a thing for Logan Jeffries... and then some. Just looking at him would leave her flushed and flustered. But that had gotten her a big fat nowhere when he'd turned down her Homecoming invitation. And she hadn't run into anyone else who made her feel that way inside since. Until she did, she'd just wait. She'd always wondered what touching Logan and being touched by him would be like, if just looking at him left her feeling that way. She'd spent many a fantasy working through that one.

"Come on," Norris said, interrupting her wool-gathering. "You've got to give me *something*."

There was her family. Talk about a soap opera. "Okay. I have twenty-two step-siblings and six half siblings. At least I think that's right."

"Holy smokes." Norris sat up straighter. "How'd that happen?"

"Mom's on husband number six. Dad's with his fifth wife."

Norris whistled beneath her breath. "Your family could have its own soap opera."

"Or a really bad reality TV show," Jenna said with a laugh. But for the grace of God that had never happened. All she'd ever wanted was a nice stable home environment—to just stay put in one spot for a while. At least her mother had been considerate enough to consistently remarry within the same school district until Jenna had graduated.

"That's perfect—just the kind of thing I was looking for." Norris snapped her notebook shut. "Okay, well, I think that covers it. I'll want to do a follow-up story when the new place is open for business." Norris tucked her notepad and pen into her pocket and stood, heading for the door. Norris was nice enough not to smoke in Jenna's little business space and even if the interview hadn't been over, Jenna knew the other woman was jonesing for a nicotine hit.

"Cool. Merrilee's planned a ribbon cutting and as mayor, she's booked the first appointment. I'll see you tomorrow at ten for your mani/pedi." Norris had insisted on doing the interview outside of her appointment. She didn't believe in mixing business and pleasure.

They both stepped out onto the sidewalk.

"See you then," Norris said, taking off as if she was running late for a day-after Christmas clearance sale. She always looked as if she was running late to something. Jenna figured it must've been all those years in the news business.

Jenna's event notification went off on her cell phone. Perfect timing. She'd be right on time to meet Nelson over at the new spa.

Bundling up, she blew Tama a kiss and headed out the door. Strolling down the sidewalk, her interview fresh on her brain, she thought, for about the millionth time, how much she loved it here. She waved at Nancy and Leo Perkins as she passed the dry goods store. Petey, driving past in his beat up Suburban, blew the horn at her.

For the first time in her life, she almost felt settled. There was still something that niggled at her, a dissatisfaction of some sort, but she was sure once the business was finished and she moved into her own place—the apartment above her shop—that would disappear as well. Then she'd know complete happiness.

Logan looked over the reports, months in the making, regarding their expansion in Alaska, spread in front of him on the round mahogany table. His father, as CEO of JMC, Inc—Jeffries Mining Consolidated—commanded a corner office with an impressive view of the Atlanta skyline twenty miles south of them.

Davis Jeffries, his gray hair cropped close and wearing his customary Brooks Brother's suit and monogrammed cuff links, read through documents his secretary had brought in unrelated to their meeting, while they waited on Martina and Kyle—Logan's cousins—to arrive. His father had never been one to waste time on small talk. Martina, Logan's age, handled IT while Kyle, two years their junior, worked the field operations side of the business.

Logan leaned back in the padded leather chair, the same as he had countless times before and studied the same picture he always studied on the paneled wall opposite the seat he always sat in.

Great-grandfather Jebediah Jeffries, the company founder who started out as a prospector in the north Georgia mountains and had struck gold, stared at him from the framed portrait, his stern gray gaze unflinching, shrewd. Ever since Logan had been old enough to remember, the old man had seemed to be holding him to some standard. He was thirty now and it still felt as if his ancestor was somehow measuring him.

Logan looked back to the spread sheets on the table. He'd reviewed the company cash flow and financials prior to the meeting, not that he didn't already know what was there. He always knew. It was his job to know. He'd taken over as Chief Financial Officer when his uncle Lewis, Martina's and Kyle's father, had died in a car accident. Logan had been being groomed to eventually fill that position when Lewis retired, so it was no surprise. The board had decided Logan was ready for the position when Lewis met his untimely end.

Martina strode in, followed by Kyle, and they took their seats at the conference table.

Davis looked up and said without preamble. "Let's get started." He turned to his son. "How do you feel about the recommendations?"

They'd started by pinpointing six potential sites, three of which had, over the course of the past few months, been eliminated. The other three were ranked as a first, second and third choice. Logan had watched the developing reports with interest once Good Riddance had been identified as a contender, aware that Jenna Rathburne lived there now. After months of evaluation, once a decision was reached today, things would progress quickly.

"I think we'll see a nice return on this. Acquisitions worked up the numbers for the buy-out. The residents of Good Riddance, Alaska, are about to hit the jackpot with what we're going to offer them for the town." Good Riddance had been recommended as the first choice. "No one there is starving but neither are they fast-tracking." JMC could make them all rich beyond their wildest dreams. With the company's offer, the townspeople could relocate to wherever they chose and do whatever they wanted.

Then again, the company stood to make whatever money they spent back ten-fold. Sleepy little Good Riddance, Alaska, literally sat atop a gold mine.

Logan pointed to the bottom line on the financials. "Last year, it would've been cost prohibitive but given this new technology, it's now a good deal."

Davis turned his attention to Martina. "What about your end?"

"From an IT standpoint, Barton, our second choice, is actually preferable. But we can work with Good Riddance."

Davis nodded. "Kyle?"

"Barton's not bad, but Good Riddance is better."

After asking a few more questions, Davis finally nodded. "Then let's make an offer for Good Riddance." He looked at Logan. "Are you sending Chaz?"

Charles "Chaz" Fischer usually handled the actual approach and buyout negotiations. Not this time, however.

"I'm going to handle this one," Logan said.

"You?" Kyle said. "You never leave the office."

"Exactly. The negotiations should take a couple of days, tops. Once it's wrapped up, I'd like to take some vacation time. I've always been interested in Alaska." That was true enough. He'd always been fascinated by the state. And then there was Jenna. He'd kept up with her through a mutual friend on Facebook. And back in the day, she'd fascinated him as well.

What were the odds his company would wind up

buying out the tiny little bush town she'd moved to, on the other side of the continent?

Davis concluded the meeting but asked Kyle to stay to discuss equipment updates. Martina and Logan stepped out into the carpeted hall.

"I had lunch with Aunt Laura today," Martina said.

Logan raised an eyebrow in inquiry. If his mother was "doing" lunch, there was an ulterior motive.

"Yes, she's at it again. She wants me to find you someone *suitable*. I thought about telling her I could hook you up with my friend who's a stripper just to watch her pass out." Martina grinned. Logan's cousin possessed a quirky sense of humor he really appreciated. They both knew none of her friends were strippers—at least Logan didn't think they were. "Just giving you the head's up, cuz. Now that you've hit the big three-oh and got the big title, it's time for you to pony up and contribute to the Jeffries legacy establishing the company's future leader. Of course, you'll have to walk a suitable girl down the aisle in some expensive matrimonial display first."

Logan shook his head. "I can find my own dates, thanks."

"Except you've been busy with work and finishing up your MBA. Bottom line, you're not moving fast enough in that direction to suit your parental unit. When you get back from Alaska, be ready to look over the brood mares I line up for you while you're gone. Make it easier for me. Do you prefer blondes, brunettes or redheads?"

Strictly because they'd just discussed Good Riddance, Jenna came to mind. He was absolutely certain, however, that the outgoing Jenna who did nails for a living wasn't his mother's definition of suitable.

"I'd have to say blondes."

JENNA OPENED THE FRONT door of the new spa and her future home and stepped inside. Even though it was just an empty shell at this point, it was her empty shell.

Home. She grinned and twirled across the open expanse. Breathless, she stopped and looked around her, envisioning the place a month from now.

There was still a faint sense of uneasiness inside her she couldn't quite shake. When Sven got her place framed in, maybe then she'd shake this feeling.

Thick glass windows offered views of the large evergreens on two sides and Good Riddance on the other two sides.

The materials for the interior lay stacked at the back of the building. She heard Sven, the construction foreman, talking to one of his guys outside. They should finish up the rear exterior today and not a minute too soon. Snow was fast on its way and it was already colder than Sven liked to have his crew working outside. That was the reason she hadn't popped around out back. She didn't want to slow them down.

She liked the big third-generation Swede in charge of her construction. Well, she didn't like him *that* way. He was a good-looking guy and they got along great together, but there were no sparks there. Just to test the waters, she and Sven had kissed once. Once had been enough. Not that it was awful. Sven was actually a very competent kisser, but she wasn't looking for competence. Well, actually, she supposed she did want competence, but she also wanted overwhelming passion and that just hadn't been happening. So, friends they were.

Tomorrow they'd start the interior construction. She pulled her coat tighter around her, envisioning the walls in place and the waterfall that would be in the reception area. It wouldn't be a big spa but it would be nice. And like most Good Riddance business owners, she'd live upstairs. It was definitely cheaper to build up rather than out.

The front door opened and Nelson Sisnuket stepped inside. His long, raven-black hair was pulled back in its customary ponytail, held with a leather strip.

Nelson was a good friend. Most people liked Jenna well enough, but very few people "got" her. Nelson did.

"Hi, Jenna."

"Hey, Nelson," she said, giving him a quick hug.

Nelson was way cool. Jenna loved him. Well, not love-love, even though she'd tested those waters, too. But they'd both quickly figured out they were meant to just be friends. That was happening to Jenna a lot these days. "I appreciate you making time for this."

Nelson was one busy guy. He worked at the local doctor's office as an assistant and office manager. He was also a shaman-in-training for his tribe. The tribe's rule against interracial dating had made a relationship between them impossible, even if there *had* been chemistry.

Nelson would make a great shaman, Jenna thought. There was just something about him, a centered-ness. When she was a kid, she and one of her step-sisters, Lillith, had discovered a secret place on Lillith's grandpa's farm, one they'd returned to every chance they got. A copse of trees surrounded a quiet stream fed by an underground spring. Jenna had loved that stream for its calmness, clarity and constancy. Hanging out with Nelson always reminded her of that place and dipping her toes into the sun-dappled water.

"No problem. I'm glad to do this for you," he said. "The clinic's been slow but with the weather change, we'll get busier," he said. "How are you?"

It was one of those questions people asked without caring about the answer. But Nelson really wanted to know.

Had it been anyone else, Jenna would've given

them a pat answer. But this was Nelson. "I've had a touch of the funk," she said.

While she explained her theory behind feeling unsettled, Nelson reached inside his jacket and pulled out an animal-skin pouch. Squatting on his haunches, he placed it on the floor, unfolded it and pulled out what looked like a seriously oversized cigar. It was actually a bundle of sage tied with string.

Jenna had asked Nelson to "smudge" her new building to clear any negative energy before Sven and his crew started on the interior. It was a native tradition Nelson performed regularly at the clinic, cleansing the space. And Jenna wanted as much good energy in her own place as possible.

She and Nelson walked to the farthermost corner of the building. He struck a match and held the flame to the end of the bundle until it began to burn. Smoke curled into the air and he spoke a few prayers, raising and lowering the sage stick at the same time.

"I don't know," she concluded once he'd finished. "You ever feel like things are going right but something just feels off?"

He peered at her, seeming to see some place inside her. Nelson had a way of doing that. She was pretty sure it was that shaman thing he was training for. "Yes?" he said.

They leaned against the back wall, the scent of burnt sage wafting around them.

"I can't quite put my finger on it," Jenna said. "I

love living here. Even though I have a business in Marietta, it's never felt the same as this." She held out her arms to the empty room and circled slowly. "This is my home. How cool is that? So why do I have this…I don't know how to describe it."

"Kind of an empty spot inside?"

"Well, yeah. Maybe a little."

"Perhaps you are ready to find your mate."

"No. You can take that back to the drawing board. I'm just peachy keen on my own."

She'd been a strike-out queen when it came to relationships. That, however, was no small wonder considering both her parents' track record. If she rolled with the whole concept of genetics, neither of her parents seemed to possess the ability to success- fully settle down. Apparently it was a defect she'd inherited. So she'd been cautious, determined not to bounce from relationship to relationship. She'd been holding out for something special.

However, at this point, she figured she probably qualified as the world's oldest virgin. Still, she wasn't about to rush into anything just for the sake of saying she had a boyfriend or that she'd done *it*. She wanted it to mean something. She refused to be a conquest, or worse yet, simply an available warm body in a bed.

"But I think a relationship is what you're miss- ing." Nelson could be quietly persistent. And they both knew he didn't mean a relationship between the two of them.

She loved Nelson and most of the time he got it right but not this time. Nope. She finally had what she'd wanted her entire life—stability and a sense of belonging. She eyed Nelson. "I think you're projecting. Maybe you're feeling like you want a girlfriend."

He shrugged, saying nothing, his dark eyes probing.

Jenna shook her head. "Nuh-uh. I'm doing just fine on my own."

Another relationship to screw up was the last thing she needed.

2

"WE'RE ALMOST THERE," SAID the brunette puddle-jumper pilot named Juliette who'd picked Logan up in Anchorage.

His heart beat faster as he looked out over the buildings below. Jenna was down there. He was possibly minutes from seeing her again for the first time in twelve years.

The woman confounded him. He couldn't seem to shake the attraction he'd always had for her, especially considering that little Homecoming incident.

And dammit, he'd dreamed about her almost every night since his secretary had booked this trip. Steamy, sultry erotic dreams where he was making love to her and she was beneath him, on top of him, beside him. The hell of it was, every time he had one of those dreams, it ended just before either of them climaxed. He'd wake up in a sweat with a raging hard-on. How could a woman he hadn't seen in years, one he hadn't even really known, affect him this way? It was enough to drive a man insane.

Surely it was just a matter of pride. He told himself he was eager to see her so she could see the geek she'd tried to prank had turned out okay. There was something to be said for the old adage that success was the best revenge. Not that he wanted any kind of revenge but he did feel the need for her to see first-hand just how successful he'd become.

It might be a family business, but nothing had been a given. If anything, carrying the Jeffries name meant you had to prove yourself that much more, to live up to the family legacy. And it came with both personal and professional expectations. He really wasn't surprised his mother had enlisted Martina in finding him a potential spouse. Marriage and pro-creation fell next on the Jeffries obligation list.

Besides, he was admittedly looking forward to playing the hero. He was about to make the dreams come true of everyone living in Jenna's little town. That was the only reason he wanted to see her.

It was *not* because he still had a thing for her after all this time. That would qualify as irrational. And it wouldn't make any sense. Logan didn't do irrational or senseless. No, he just wanted Jenna to see he'd done well for himself.

True to the satellite images, topographical maps and reports he'd read, a road bisected two rows of buildings. Twilight and snow encompassed the town ringed by towering evergreens. The ruggedness echoed the set designs for the western movies he'd always liked so much as a kid, except this town wasn't located in the middle of a desert.

"I'll have us down in a second," Juliette, the pilot, said. He glanced over at the brunette.

"Good deal."

She radioed for clearance to land. Really, there was something warped about his thinking. Juliette was very attractive, obviously intelligent from the conversation they'd had on the way out about flying and Alaska, and about his age.

He wasn't remotely interested in her other than as the pilot getting him to Good Riddance. Instead he couldn't get Jenna Rathburne out of his head. Those dreams had definitely screwed with his head and his rational thought processes.

A few minutes later they were on the ground, snow falling thick and fast from the heavy blanket of gray clouds.

"Here we are. Hopefully your luggage will make it sooner rather than later," Juliette said.

Logan nodded and climbed out of the plane. The snow swirled around him, crisp, cold and fresh. In the distance, the air rang with the sound of barking dogs interspersed with children's laughter along with the unmistakable hum of a diesel engine. He shivered and zipped his jacket. It was damn cold out here.

Because he'd been traveling, he had dressed

lighter. Still, he'd dressed the part, trading business suits and business casual for boots, jeans and a flannel shirt he'd worn on trips to field operations in the past. He'd fully planned to retrieve his heavier jacket and gloves once he'd arrived in Anchorage. He'd arrived but his suitcase hadn't. He really didn't like it when things didn't go according to plan, but there'd been nothing he could do about it.

Logan walked beside Juliette across the open expanse between the small runway and the log building, heading toward a door next to a sign that read Good Riddance Air Strip and Bed and Breakfast. On the far right side of the building, another sign outside yet another door proclaimed, "Welcome to Gus's," exactly as it had been described in the scouting report. A few months ago, one of Chaz's team had been sent in, as a tourist, to assess the area, the people, the infrastructure and then compile a report which was part of the recommendations criteria.

Logan followed the pilot into the toasty-warm room, pausing inside to wipe his feet on the mat and brush the snow off his shoulders and hair. An older woman, about his mother's age, dressed in jeans and a lace-trimmed flannel shirt, stepped forward to greet him.

"You must be Mr. Jeffries." Her soft Southern accent once again brought his mother to mind, although his mother wouldn't be caught dead in anything flannel. "I'm Merrilee Danville Swenson. As town founder and mayor, I'd like to welcome you to Good Riddance, where you can leave behind what ails you."

Juliette had mentioned the town motto on the flight in. *That* had not been in the reports package.

Her handshake was firm and to the point. Logan immediately liked her. Her cooperation would be pivotal in buying out the town. He offered his most charming smile. "I'm pleased to meet you, Mrs. Swenson, and I'm pleased to be here."

He had been surprised to discover a woman had founded this place out in the middle of the wilderness. However, it was exactly that pioneering spirit that would serve her well in relocating her little town. He even had a couple of locations to suggest when they sat down to discuss business. He planned to do that tomorrow. He wanted to establish a rapport with her and meet some of the townspeople before he broached the subject of the buy-out.

She smiled. "Call me Merrilee. Everyone does."

"And I'm Logan." They were off to a good start.

"Good. We don't stand on ceremony here. There's fresh coffee—" she indicated a small table set up as a beverage station "—help yourself. And don't be shy with the oatmeal cookies, either. Juliette and I need to go over a few things so we can get her back in the air and then I'll be right with you."

"Sure. Take your time."

While Juliette went over paperwork with the

older woman, he poured a cup of coffee, snagged a cookie…and then another since he was starving, and studied the room.

Not that he hadn't expected it but this was vastly different from the office space he worked in every day. Photographs covered one of the chinked-log walls. There was a love seat and two armchairs clustered around a television set in one corner. Flannel curtains hung at the windows and a braided rug covered a large expanse of the wood floor.

He blew on his drink and sipped. Strong and dark, it blazed a warm trail through him. And something smelled damn good.

He concurred with the recommendation put forth in the report. The airstrip and this building would be an asset as the mining operation was set up. It sat far enough on the perimeter to be functional, while the rest of the buildings would, in all probability, be bulldozed down. This, however, would make the perfect headquarters site, especially with the attached restaurant. They couldn't have asked for anything better.

A pot-bellied stove sat to the right of the room. An old man with a long white beard sat in a rocking chair on one side of a chess set, muttering to himself. The rocker on the opposite side sat empty.

"Enjoy your stay," Juliette said, sending a friendly smile his way as she headed back out the door.

"Will do. Thanks again."

When the door closed behind the pilot, Merrilee looked toward the old man and shook her head, a gleam of sadness in her eyes. "That's Dwight Simmons. He's harmless, just a little lost. His chess partner Jeb Taylor passed away this summer. Dwight still hasn't quite figured out what to do without Jeb. The two of them spent their days playing chess and arguing, but they were like family to one another."

Logan nodded and murmured something noncommittal, unsure what to say in the face of the old man's loss.

"Now let's take care of you," Merrilee said, patting him on the arm. Logan had steadfastly tried to push Jenna to the back of his mind but now he was within proverbial spitting distance of her and it took every ounce of willpower for him not to ask Ms. Swenson—make that Merrilee—where he could find Jenna. That would go a long way in taking care of one of his items on his to-do list. "I understand you've had a bit of a rough travel day," Merrilee said.

She'd been notified of his flight delays so the last leg of his trip could be rescheduled.

Logan nodded. "It's been a long day. A wreck shut down the expressway this morning. I could see the airport. I was half a mile from the exit, but I couldn't get there, which meant I missed the direct flight." As a result, he'd had to fly around his ass to get to Anchorage by way of New York, then Los Angeles, and finally on to Anchorage. Somewhere between

Atlanta, New York, LA and Anchorage, his luggage had gone missing.

"Would you rather freshen up in your room first? I've left a few toiletries as I understand your luggage didn't make it here with you. Or do you want to grab some grub next door first?"

Between the innumerable delays that had left him hurrying up and waiting, he hadn't grabbed breakfast at the airport the way he'd intended to, nor had he had the opportunity to snag any food at Atlanta's Hartsfield-Jackson terminal. He'd had to sprint through the airport to make the flight, which had then spent an hour sitting out on the tarmac waiting for clearance before take off. He'd traveled often enough to know shit happened, but not usually this much shit all in one day.

"I need to wash up a bit, but then I'm ready to eat. Whatever it is smells great." The scent alone had him salivating. The cookies had helped but he was still hungry. For good measure, his stomach growled in agreement.

"No worries," Merrilee said with a bright smile. "I'll show you to your room and then they'll fix you right up next door."

She headed toward a stairway on the other side of the office. Logan followed her up to the second floor.

"I understand one of my former schoolmates lives

here. Jenna Rathburne," Logan said as they climbed the stairs.

Merrilee stopped and turned to face him on the stairs, surprise on her face. "You know Jenna? She didn't tell us you'd be coming."

"I haven't contacted her. I thought I'd look her up when I got here."

"Oh! A surprise! I'm sure she'll be tickled pink."

Logan wasn't so sure at all. In fact, he felt a fairly alien moment of uncertainty as to exactly how Jenna would respond when she saw him. "We went to the same high school." He knew he sounded guarded.

"We all just love that girl to pieces. She's one of those rare women who's as beautiful on the inside as she is on the outside. She's got a heart of gold."

Logan was saved from responding, which was good because he didn't know what to say anyway, when Merrilee opened a door at the top of stairs. "Here you are." He stepped behind her into a room that was charming and inviting, but damn cold.

"We're having a little problem with the heating upstairs," Mrs. Swenson said.

"I'll be fine." As soon as his luggage containing his thermal underwear and thick socks arrived.

Aside from the cold, he immediately liked the room. As with the downstairs, it had log walls and lace-trimmed flannel curtains. An iron headboard and footboard were painted a light cream color. A homey quilt covered the mattress while a washstand, complete with antique pitcher and bowl, stood in one corner. A crocheted doily, much like those found in his grandmother's house, topped the nightstand. Light from a bedside lamp pooled across a rag rug and the pegged wooden floor. The welcoming scent of cinnamon and apples hung faint in the room.

"The bathroom is down the hall at the other end of the landing. Just holler if you need anything."

Food first and then directions to Jenna. See, he wasn't desperate to see her at all. He'd eat first.

He was, after all, fully in control.

"HE'S CLEANING UP NOW AND then he's heading over to Gus's," Merrilee said.

Jenna's heart was racing in her chest. "Logan Jeffries?" Her voice came out all squeaky.

"Uh-huh," Merrilee said. "How many Logan's do you know from high school, sweetie?" Merrilee's question held a teasing note.

"Only one." And he was here. Logan Jeffries was right down the street, here in Good Riddance, Alaska. Dear God.

"What's he doing here?"

"Well, I have no idea. The only thing he brought up was you."

For one heart-stopping moment, a crazy thought passed through her mind…. No. Uh-uh. That was ridiculous. Over the top. Wildly romantic.

Jenna really didn't know what Logan did for a living, so she had no clue what else could've brought him here. But it couldn't be her…could it?

Merrilee continued. "He was going to surprise you. I hate to spoil that but I thought you might want a heads up. Most women do when a good-looking man is going to drop in on them."

Surprised didn't begin to describe it. Honestly, Jenna felt kind of weak at the knees. Then again, Logan had always affected her that way. "He still looks good?"

"Well, sugar, I have no idea what he looked like back in the day, but he looks mighty fine now. Tall, broad-shouldered, dark hair, pretty brown eyes and, never tell Bull I said it but, a mouth a woman could only think of as kissable. A little reserved and formal, but nice nonetheless."

Butterflies seemed to take flight in Jenna's stomach releasing a sweet heat she hadn't felt in a long time. Logan had always had a great mouth. A sensual shiver ran through her. She'd fantasized numerous times about him and his sexy mouth—on her lips, her breasts, the inside of her wrist, the inside of her thighs. She'd imagined what it would feel like, how he would taste…and it had never gotten her anywhere but aroused and frustrated. She might be a virgin but she had all the working parts and certainly the desire.

"Oh, Lord."

She didn't realize she'd spoken aloud until Merrilee chuckled on the other end of the line.

"Well, Ms. Jenna, is there something you'd like to tell me about Logan Jeffries? Because I'm thinking he's not just another anybody from back home."

Jenna glanced in the mirror. This sweater and blue jeans had been fine when she'd put it on this morning but not now, not if she was going to be seeing Logan for the first time in forever.

"Jenna?"

Jenna pulled her attention back to the conversation, away from her reflection in the mirror and the knot of anticipation and nervousness lodged in her mid-section.

"Oh, yeah. Sorry. What was that?" She stuck the Closed sign on the front of the door and was already shrugging into her jacket. She pulled on her gloves and hat and wound a pink scarf around her neck, her hands slightly unsteady.

There was no option, she needed to hotfoot it home to redo her make-up and hair and change clothes. She'd be double-damned if Logan Jeffries wasn't going to eat his heart out when he saw her again. She wasn't holding a grudge exactly but she did have some feminine pride.

Tama met her at the door, ready to go with her. She supposed he was ready for a change of scenery.

"What's the deal with this guy?" Merrilee said,

opening the door of the shop. "Because you're definitely rattled."

"Well, it's not every day that someone from back home shows up," Jenna hedged as she stepped out into the dancing snow flurries and closed the door behind her.

"Right. Now tell me the rest of the story. Because I know you well enough to know there's 'a rest of the story' somewhere in there."

There was no hiding anything from Merrilee. Then again, it wasn't as if her past was a state secret or anything. She came clean. "It's water under the bridge, really. I asked him to escort me to Homecoming, back in high school. He turned me down. It's not a big deal." Well, okay, it had been devastating at the time and it still stung just a little. That was why she was heading home.

"He turned you down?" Merrilee sounded flatteringly shocked.

Jenna dodged a sled dog curled up on the sidewalk in front of the dry goods store, waving at Nancy who was dusting shelves inside. Nancy was a good, regular customer and she had nice nails to work with. Jenna never could remember whether they'd lived in Michigan or Wisconsin before they retired to Good Riddance. "He did, indeed."

"Then he's not as smart as he looks."

"Oh, no. He's really, really smart, like supersmart." He'd been the debate team captain and she'd carried the most incredible torch for him even though she knew she wasn't his type. Translation—she wasn't brainiac enough for him.

"Honey, if he turned you down, he couldn't be all that bright."

Jenna laughed as she let herself into the cabin she rented from the town's former doctor who'd moved to San Francisco last year. There'd been no need to unlock the door because in Good Riddance, no one bothered. Although Jenna was still enough of a city girl to lock hers before she went to bed at night. "Trust me, he's brilliant."

"Well, smart or not," Merrilee said, "it looks as if he's temporarily dropped smack dab back into your life. He's booked the next five days."

A funny feeling coiled through her, chased by Nelson's words earlier that she was missing someone in her life.

No, no and no. She didn't need anyone, and if she did, it sure as heck wouldn't be Logan. He was only here temporarily and that suited her just fine. Sure, she'd had a tremendous thing for him back in the day and perhaps he'd always been the guy she'd always wondered about, but that part of her life was long gone.

A whole lot of water had passed under that bridge. *If* she wanted a man in her life, it certainly wouldn't be Logan Jeffries.

<u>3</u>

LOGAN CHEWED AND SWALLOWED the last bite of his caribou stew. Within seconds the waitress, a ponytailed blonde named Teddy, was at his booth. "The daily special comes with seconds. Would you like some more stew? More rolls? Another glass of water?"

"It was delicious," he said. And it had been. "But I'm full. I'll just take the check when you have a minute."

"Sure thing."

Gus's, the restaurant housed in the same building as the bed and breakfast but separated by a wall with a connecting door, was an interesting place for sure. Once again, it reminded him of a scene out of an old western. A bar, complete with the brass footrest, fronted two-thirds of the wall beside the connecting door. He had to smile at the moose head wearing a pair of sunglasses mounted over the bar's back wall.

The other third was devoted to the kitchen area,

open to the rest of the room except for a high counter. Restrooms, pool tables, a dartboard a jukebox, and a small stage occupied the area to the left of the door. The remaining two walls were lined with booths like the one he was occupying near the bar. The room's center held a number of tables and chairs. Across the room, another door was tucked into the wall.

The place was busy considering it was late in the afternoon but it was already dark outside. He'd gotten several curious glances since he'd wandered in half an hour ago. He'd overheard a smattering of conversations and he should've attempted getting to know some of the residents, but now that he was here, he couldn't seem to get Jenna off of his mind.

There was only one thing to do. He needed to look her up so he could cross her off his list. Drop in, say hello, satisfy his curiosity and then get on with the task at hand. It was a simple and straightforward solution to what shouldn't have even been a problem to begin with.

The waitress returned with his check. "You sure I can't get you a piece of pie? Lucky made chocolate cream this morning. It's yummy."

He smiled. "Thanks, but I'll pass."

The sooner he tracked down Jenna, the better. Then he could focus on what really counted, offering everyone in Good Riddance a financial security they'd probably never known before.

Leaving his money on the table, he grabbed the

jacket he was very glad he'd worn and headed back to the airstrip. Merrilee Swenson sat at her desk, filling out what looked like an official form. He knew from experience that a boatload of paperwork came with any business, even running a small airstrip like this one.

She looked up as he crossed the room, his shoes echoing on the wooden floor. "How was your meal?"

"Excellent."

"Glad to hear it. We pride ourselves on the food at Gus's. It may be the only restaurant in town, but we think it's one of the best in the state."

Civic pride had been heavily weighted in the scouting report and factored into the buy-out offer.

"I haven't had caribou stew before, but it was certainly tasty."

"Wait until you try the moose pot pie. And you'll have to check out karaoke night on Thursday. It's a lot of fun."

Smiling, Logan shook his head. "I can't say I'm big on karaoke."

"You will be by then. There's not a lot of entertainment to be found in Good Riddance. It's more fun than you might think." She shoved her ink pen behind one ear. "By the way, your luggage should arrive tomorrow morning. It's coming into Anchorage on a red-eye flight. Don't ask me how but it wound up in Tulsa."

"I've heard of stranger things happening." He

chuckled, aiming for casual. "I thought I'd look Jenna up now that my stomach rumblings won't embarrass me. Where do you think I'll find her?"

"Oh, she'll be at Curl's. She's got a nail business going there. Well, actually, she's building a little day spa on the outskirts of town, but for now she's operating out of the front of Curl's place."

He was aware of Curl's and Jenna's nail business. The spa must be a relatively new development, at least within the past six months, since it hadn't been on the reports he'd seen. But it wasn't anything he couldn't handle and counter. He didn't want to come across as too in-the-know. "Curl's?"

"Curl owns the taxidermy, barber shop and mortuary."

"I'm guessing Jenna's business is part of the barber shop instead of the mortuary."

Merrilee grinned. "They're all together. But yes, Jenna's business is in the front where the barber shop and hair salon are. The taxidermy and mortuary are in the back. We're big on one-stop shopping here," Merrilee said with a wink. "Go out the front door, hang a left and it's down on the right. You can't miss it."

Logan returned her smile. "I think it'd be hard to miss anything with just one street." He headed toward the front door.

"True enough. Jenna's pretty hard to miss," Merrilee said with an arch look.

His gut was already knotted at the thought. "I'm sure."

He stepped outside and the cold slammed him. Dammit, he was so disconcerted, he hadn't thought to put on his jacket. He shrugged into and zipped it, although it was far too thin for this weather. Shoving his hands in the pockets, he started down the sidewalk.

There *was* a charm about the place that was hard to put his finger on. Despite the cold, the town seemed to radiate warmth—from the patrons at Gus's to Merrilee, herself. Light spilled out of the storefronts along the single thoroughfare, reflecting off of the snow which kept it from being too dark, even without streetlights.

He stepped around a grey and black dog curled up on the sidewalk, seemingly impervious to the frigid air and snow. The unmistakable aroma of wood smoke mingled with the scent of evergreens. Working here wouldn't be a hardship for the crew the company would send in to man the operation.

He exchanged hellos with a man he passed on the sidewalk. The guy sported a full beard—right now Logan wouldn't mind a beard to keep his face warm—and a fur hat which Logan had no doubt was the genuine article.

A group of kids chased one another down the sidewalk, their laughter and yelling ringing in the air. A dirty pick-up truck sporting a set of antlers as a hood ornament drove down the street past him. The few cars and trucks parked along the street were un-washed and obviously had years and miles on them.

And then he was there. Across the street was Curl's—the name and services were written across the picture window fronting the business—but more telling was the woman he saw through the window.

Jenna stood talking to two women. A tall blonde woman towered over Jenna and another woman with long dark hair. But it was Jenna who held his atten-tion. His heart thumped against his rib cage and de-spite the cold, a fine sheen of sweat popped up on his skin. If anything, she was even lovelier than he remembered. Her Facebook photo hadn't done her justice.

He stood on the sidewalk and drank in the sight of her, like a man viewing one of the world's natu-ral wonders for the first time. Her blond hair hung slightly past her shoulders. Animated, she smiled and laughed with the other women, her face glow-ing. She'd always radiated vitality.

A light pink sweater dress clung to and outlined all of her curves. Somewhere between graduation and now, she'd obviously had a breast enhancement. Logan preferred the real thing and as far as he was concerned, she'd been damn near perfect in high school. Still, women were going to do what women were going to do. Dana, Kyle's secretary, had bought herself new breasts. Silicone or not, Jenna took his breath away.

He stood stock-still, feeling paralyzed, hearing his racing pulse pound in his ears.

"Hey, buddy. Are you okay? You need directions or something?" a guy around Logan's age and height asked, rousing Logan out of his trance, stupor or whatever you wanted to call it. Idiocy seemed to fit the bill as well.

"Uh, yeah. I was just getting my bearings."

"That shouldn't take long, considering the size of our town," the other guy said with a friendly grin, shoving his gloved hand in Logan's direction. "We haven't met. I'm Dalton Saunders. I hear Juliette brought you in earlier today. I'm the other pilot in town."

Logan shook the guy's hand. "Logan Jeffries. Pleased to meet you."

Dalton eyed Logan's thin jacket sympathetically. "I also hear they redirected your luggage. I won't hold you up. See you around."

"Sure. Nice to meet you."

Dalton took off with a jaunty step, whistling beneath his breath. Logan crossed the street, eager to get this over with before he could make an even bigger fool of himself. Then again, it wasn't the first time he'd stood around, gaping at Jenna.

"THANKS AGAIN, JENNA. They look great," Donna said, admiring her new set of nails. Donna ran the small engine repair shop in town. Even with gloves on, it was tough on her hands. Solar nails had turned out to be Donna's best bet.

Once upon a time, long before Jenna had met her, Donna had been Don and apparently quite a football star at a Midwestern university. Donna was one of Jenna's favorite people in town. Jenna admired anyone who had the courage to follow their heart, regardless of the censure they encountered, not that Donna found any here. That was one of the things Jenna loved about Good Riddance—everyone accepted everyone else for who and what they were.

"They do look good," Jenna said, echoing Donna's admiration even while she felt all tangled up inside. Logan was out there. She *felt* him, *sensed* him. It had been that way in high school as well. It was as if some radar went off inside her. Then she'd turn a corner and he'd be standing there. She had that same internal alarm going off now.

Jangled or not, Jenna turned to Ellie Lightfoot. "Thanks for stopping by, Ellie. I'm looking forward to working with you."

Donna laughed. "I'm looking forward to you working on me."

· Ellie, her long dark hair hanging down her back in a single plait, smiled shyly. "I'm looking forward to it, as well. My instructor says I have strong hands but a gentle touch—a good combination."

The native woman, around Jenna's age, was a school teacher but had spent her summer getting certified in massage. She'd approached Jenna about working in the spa and Jenna desperately needed a massage therapist. Quiet Ellie would be perfect for the job.

Jenna knew she'd dated Clint Sisnuket before Clint had found love with Tessa Bellingham. Ellie had been in twice for a mani/pedi in the past eight months but was always very quiet.

"Same time next week?" Donna said, she and Ellie heading for the door.

"Sure thing. I've got you down in my book. And Ellie, I'll see you tomorrow." Ellie was going to stop by and demo her neck massage technique for Jenna. Jenna, however, was confident that Ellie would do just fine.

Donna opened the door, stepping outside, and Jenna heard her say, "Oh, hi. You're going in?"

"Yes, thanks."

She'd recognize that voice anywhere, anytime, even if Merrilee hadn't given her a heads up that Logan was here. There was a rich, melodious quality to his voice that had always sent a shiver through her. And it still did.

And then he was standing there in front of her, and she didn't know how to identify the feelings rolling through her. The door closed behind him. The front section of Curl's wasn't spacious by any means but it seemed to shrink considerably once she and Logan were sharing the space. The universe seemed to stop and she lost herself in the depths of his brown eyes.

Silence filled the distance between them, connecting them. Time and age had changed him. His dark hair was longer than it had been years ago. It brushed his collar, a hint of a wave in the lock hanging over his forehead. She liked it.

He still had the prettiest, sexiest eyes she'd ever seen on a man, a medium-chocolate brown fringed by dark lashes. And that mouth. It was still ever so kissable, even though she'd never had the opportunity to find out firsthand.

Although she would've recognized him regardless, he did look a little different. His face had filled out, matured in a way that emphasized the strength of his square jaw. He'd been a teenage boy when she'd had such a crush on him. Now he was an extremely attractive, nicely-filled-out and all-grown-up man. Life and experience had refined his features, carved planes and angles and lines.

She felt frozen, yet on fire all at the same time.

"Jenna…" The husky note in his voice strummed through her, a key unlocking a secret, remote chamber. Hesitant, he stepped toward her. "You're even prettier than I remembered."

She'd had men compliment her before but something about his quiet words touched her. Her heart pounded so hard, surely he could hear it. The look in his eyes seared her, igniting a heat deep in her belly.

"Logan." It came out a whisper, full of an emotion she couldn't decipher at the moment.

Instinctively, without thinking it through, she moved toward him. She was a hugger by nature, but wrapping her arms around Logan's broad shoulders and feeling his warm breath against her neck made her shiver. It felt so right to be there, as if she'd finally found where she belonged.

She meant to step away, to move back but he tightened his arms around her. She wanted to stay right where she was. Slowly, deliberately Logan lowered his head, his intent evident in his thickly fringed eyes. He was going to kiss her. She could barely breathe and she thought her heart might pound out of her chest.

His breath feathered against her lips, his chest, broad and hard, scraped against her pebbled nipples. She was so ready. She'd fantasized about this moment countless times. She leaned into him, letting her eyes drift shut, anticipating the feel and taste of his lips....

Splat!

They jerked apart. Jenna and Logan both looked in the direction of the sound. The remains of a misfired snowball finished its lazy slide down the front window. Outside, kids laughed, joined by a dog barking.

Jenna was as simultaneously relieved and frustrated as she'd ever been in her life. She'd almost kissed and been kissed by Logan Jeffries. Okay, yes, she was relieved that she hadn't been caught standing in the front window of Curl's, kissing this man? On the flip side, she'd almost kissed and been kissed by Logan Jeffries!

She stepped back at the same time he did. Surprise skittered across his handsome face, as if he wasn't quite sure what had just almost happened.

Self-consciousness seemed to strike them both at the same time. Jenna glanced at the front window again. Teddy stood outside, her mouth gaping open. Jenna waved. Teddy snapped her mouth shut, grinned and waved back. She jerked her thumb over her finger mouthing, "Kids."

Jenna nodded. The kids were big on snowball fights. Getting caught in the crossfire was a common occurrence. Her standing in Curl's and nearly kissing a man, however, wasn't. Norris might think they needed a newspaper, but news spread faster here than water ran downhill. "Well, that'll be all over town before you can sneeze," Jenna said.

Logan shrugged. "I'm okay with that if you are."

The fleeting crazy idea that he might've actually came to see her danced once again through her head. Hadn't he almost kissed her?

She nodded, looking away from his intent gaze. "So," Jenna said, busying herself lining up the nail polishes that didn't need lining up, "it's been a long time." What she wanted to do was wrap her arms back around him, run her fingers through his hair and see if she was still tingling all over after he kissed her. Because she'd certainly been tingling at their near-miss.

Out of the corner of her eye, she saw Logan shove his hands in his pockets. "Yeah, it has been. I didn't make the ten-year class reunion. Did you?"

Jenna shook her head. "No. I didn't make it, either." She'd decided against it. She'd still been unsettled in her life and hadn't felt up to going and making the inevitable comparisons. The people she'd really wanted to keep up with, well, she did that through Facebook anyway. "So, you still live in Marietta?"

"I live in Atlanta, well, Vinings." Jenna knew the area which attracted upscale young professionals. Her business and apartment had been in a much less affluent part of town. "My parents are still in Marietta, though," he said.

There was pause as if neither one of them quite knew what to say next. Okay, she couldn't stand it any longer. She had to ask.

"What are you doing here?" she said.

"How'd you wind up here?" he said at the same time.

They both laughed, easing some of the tension between them. "Ladies, first," he said.

She didn't want to get into the whole Tad thing right now. She wanted to find out why the heck *he* was here. "A man. What else?"

"Oh," Logan said, a peculiar look on his face and she didn't miss his quick glance at her ring finger. Hmm, interesting.

"A man who's now out of the picture," she added. She didn't care if she was being obvious or not.

"Oh." This time he sounded altogether different.

"Your turn," she said. "What brings you here?"

He leaned against the door jamb, looking cool, confident and together. "I needed some time out of the office. The last several years have been crazy, especially since I became CFO."

Ah, she got it. He was a harried executive taking some much-needed vacation time. But wasn't Good Riddance just a little off the executive down-time list? Shouldn't he be golfing somewhere in the Caribbean. Sometimes men were so obvious. She played along. "I'm impressed." Actually, she was impressed.

She reminded herself she was CFO, CEO and COO all rolled into one. Of course, her fledgling enterprise was probably small potatoes compared to his firm. "Who do you work for?"

"JMC, Inc." That didn't ring any bells. She must've looked blank. "Jeffries Mining Consolidated."

Mining. Yes, she got it now. It all clicked into place…and made a heck of a lot more sense than thinking he'd come all this way just to look her up. It would've been nice had Merrilee had let her in on the real reason Logan was here. If she knew. Still,

Jenna was not disappointed he wasn't here to see her. Not even a little bit. Not even a smidge.

"You're here about the gold," she said, proud of her even voice and smile. There had been a guy a couple of months ago whom Merrilee had identified as a scout. Merrilee had never told the guy she was on to him, but she'd known. Heck, everyone in town knew it was just a matter of time. And apparently, the time was here. If Logan was CFO, he was the big money man. "You're here to make an offer." It wasn't a question.

He had a good poker face but she caught a glimpse of surprise nonetheless. "It's a very generous offer. No one here will ever have to work again."

Two things immediately came to mind. One, she *wanted* to work. She loved what she did and was excited about the spa she was building. Her second thought was, what would they all do if they didn't work? Sit around and look at one another?

"That sounds a little crazy to me."

"Trust me, once you all consider the possibilities, moving won't seem like such an ordeal. I've seen—"

"Whoa. Back up a bit. Did you say moving?"

He ran his hand over his head, his composure rattled. "Jenna, pretty well everyone will have to move. We'll only need a few people to run the airstrip and a couple of the other businesses."

"So, you want the town to pack up and move on?"

"Of course. That's why we'll pay everyone so handsomely."

Jenna sat down in the barber/salon chair. "You mean it."

"Absolutely."

Jenna thought about Merrilee, who had invested her heart and soul into Good Riddance. Then there was Merrilee's husband, Bull, a Vietnam vet who'd called this place home for the past twenty-something years. And how about Donna, who'd built her business and found acceptance here? Skye Shanahan had given up her medical practice in Atlanta to move here and was now happily married to quirky Dalton Saunders. And those were just a few of the people who'd built a life around Good Riddance. Poor Logan, he didn't have a clue.

Merrilee had obviously just let him have his say. Although Jenna was surprised Merrilee hadn't called Jenna to let her know. But at least now, the situation made sense. He hadn't come to look her up, to find the one that got away. Wasn't there a saying, hope springs eternal in the hearts of women and fools? If there wasn't, there should be.

"I see. And you've done this before? Bought out an entire town?"

"A couple of times. It's usually just a couple of individuals with property but yeah, we've bought out towns twice before, remote places like this. Some of the people relocated to another remote area and others took off back to the city once they had money to burn. In both cases, we improved their quality of life."

Bless his heart, he was as sincere as her mother was every time she told Jenna she'd finally met her true love—all five times. "Does your job depend on this?" She hoped not.

"Why? Don't you think everyone's going to be fairly amenable?"

"Of course." They were a friendly lot. No one was going to buy into his proposal, but they weren't going to run him out of town on the rails, either. Nope he was about to be laughed all the way home.

"Maybe, if you're not too busy, you could show me around and introduce me to some of the towns-people."

He had been the debate team captain. He was a CFO and obviously very successful. Still, he didn't have a clue. Oh, boy. And people sometimes thought *she* was an airhead.

"Sure. No problem."

4

NELSON ADMITTED IT. HE WAS in—what was the term Jenna used the other day, right—a funk.

Three months ago, they'd repainted the Good Riddance Medical Facility. Dr. Skye had insisted sunny yellow paint would help everyone deal better with the upcoming long periods of darkness. But today, not even the bright yellow walls in the waiting room/reception/book keeping area was lifting his spirits. He'd even smudged earlier, all to no avail. He was still in a negative energy spiral brought on by uncertainty. His heart was heavy with his dilemma.

How could he leave Good Riddance? But then again, if he stayed would he ever truly be fulfilled?

The door opened and Teddy stepped in, pulling him out of his musings. "See you later, Ellie," she said over her shoulder. Turning, she greeted him, "Hi, Nelson."

"Hi." He waved at Ellie, his cousin's former girl-friend, as she passed the front window.

Teddy was their last afternoon appointment. Her blond hair hung loose rather than in the ponytail she wore when she was working over at Gus's, waiting tables and helping run the kitchen.

"You saged, didn't you?" she said.

That coaxed a smile out of him. Teddy insisted on calling it saging rather than smudging. "I did."

"I like the way it smells." She wrinkled her nose. "It's much nicer than the after-effects of ammonia."

Nelson shrugged. "I've gotten used to both." In keeping with standard medical practice, he disin-fected the waiting room and exam rooms to meet standards. In keeping with native tradition, he cleansed the energy and vibrations of the same rooms on a regular basis by burning the sacred sage. It was a melding of Western and Native culture, a line he had learned to straddle early on. It was the same line he currently wrestled with crossing.

Teddy unwound her scarf from her neck, tossed it onto one of the folding chairs lining the wall and headed for the communal coffee pot Nelson kept going in the waiting room.

"Hey, Jenna's got a boyfriend in town," Teddy said as she poured a cup.

That got his attention. "Really? And how do you know he's a boyfriend?"

"Cause Jenna doesn't come close to kissing a guy

in the front window of Curl's every day. Have you
ever known that to happen?"

Nelson listened, preparing a cup of cloudberry
tea, while Teddy recounted Jenna's embrace with
the man from her past, a guy who'd flown in earlier
in the day.

He wasn't totally surprised. He'd sensed changes
in the air and then the raven, a spirit guide symbol-
izing change, had appeared before him twice now.
He hadn't been sure what kind of change was coming. But transformation or growth was a certainty.

Humans were fallible, their perceptions coloring
or distorting their reality.

The raven didn't lie. However, Nelson still needed
clarity because he had no idea if the message was intended for him or Jenna—or perhaps each of them.

He blew on his tea. Clarity would come in its own
time, the same as Jenna's man had come in his.

"I'LL BE GLAD TO INTRODUCE you around town. You'll
love it here."

Logan was fairly certain Jenna didn't get the big
picture. In fact, the glimmer in her big baby blues
indicated she found his mission amusing.

Of course, he could be wrong. Even he had to
admit he wasn't thinking clearly—at all. He felt as
out of sync now than he had when he'd stood across
the street staring at her through the window like a

fool. Maybe he was suffering from some weird form of jetlag?

Something had him out of sorts. He was always calm, cool and collected. Instead he'd almost tripped over his tongue telling her she was even prettier than he remembered. Then he damn near lost his mind and kissed her like a starving man handed a steak. If it hadn't been for that snowball landing on the window...

And the hell of it was, he still had the urge to kiss her—long, hard and deep. But it was more than an urge. It was more like a need, a hunger that was as real as when he'd sat down in front of that bowl of stew earlier. The imprint of her body against his was seared into him as was the smell of her skin, the glimmer in her eyes as she lowered her lashes. And to top it all off, her pre-emptive announcement about the gold and the buyout had shaken his normal aplomb.

Something definitely had him out of sorts.

She looked at him kind of funny and he realized he'd just been standing there, lost in thought. Thinking and talking weren't usually mutually exclusive for him. In fact, he was damn good at thinking on his feet and was known in higher circles as a top-notch negotiator. But right now he was conducting himself like a top-notch imbecile.

Still, this could work to his advantage. Jenna had agreed to introduce him around town. Perfect.

According to Merrilee, everyone loved Jenna, so it stood to reason he'd be well-received if he was with her. And, as a bonus, he got to spend time with her. He had to admit he was as fascinated by her now as he had been years ago. Aside from the fact that she was pretty, there was something about her that was different, something he couldn't quite put his finger on. That bugged him. He didn't like leaving things, people or situations open-ended.

"Great." He looked around the room devoid of customers. "Depending on your schedule, I'm flexible."

She ran a manicured nail down an open appointment book on a small desk that also held a laptop and phone. There was something wickedly sensual about that simple movement which sent another wave of heat through him. That was rich—a heat wave in Alaska in October.

It seemed as if all his brain cells wanted to focus on—or seemed capable of focusing on—was the remembered feel of her pressed against him, of wondering what it would be like to have her run that fingernail over his bare chest, down his belly, circle his... He slammed on the mental brakes. Blood pooled hot and heavy below his belt. Madness lay in that direction, if not sure embarrassment.

"I've got one more appointment," she said, pursing her lips. He really wished she wouldn't do that, even though it was obviously contemplative rather than an invitation. "Wait, no, Nancy cancelled and I forgot to mark it off. She and Leo own the dry goods store two doors down, but you probably know that, don't you?" He did so he nodded. "They got in an early shipment. You wouldn't think it, but trust me, that will *wreck* Nancy's cuticles. There wasn't any point in a mani until she finished unpacking boxes and stocking shelves."

Logan found himself smiling, unwillingly charmed by her...ingenuity. "I do trust you on that point. I have no idea what would or wouldn't wreck a cuticle. That's your expertise."

"Then come on. I need to check on the interior construction for my spa." Her smile seemed to brighten the room by about sixty-watts. "Well, I don't really need to check but I'd like to check." She eyed his jacket. "It's on the other end of town and it's pretty cold out there. Are you up for the walk?"

First, there was no way he was about to admit he might be cold. Never let them see you sweat, never second guess yourself and never admit a weakness was the motto instilled in a Jeffries from birth. Second, he seriously doubted being cold was a remote possibility, regardless of the weather conditions, if he was with her. There was something about Jenna that notched his internal thermostat up several degrees. "I'm definitely up for it."

The second the words left his mouth, he realized how they sounded...and she did as well. Jenna blushed, a whoosh of color that touched from her neck to her hairline. "The walk," he said, which really only made it worse because then she glanced down to the front of his jeans. "I'm up for the walk."

"Right," she said. "Of course." She pulled a fuzzy pink and white scarf off of a peg hanger on the wall. "It doesn't exactly match your outfit but if you'd like to borrow it, it's yours." She held it out to him.

It was sweet of her to offer, but he wasn't wearing that scarf, at least not in this lifetime. "Thanks, but I'll be fine."

She wrapped the scarf around her neck and grabbed a soft matching cap. "I'm guessing you'll pass on the hat as well."

He laughed. "Yeah."

Jenna grinned, putting it on her head and pulling it down past her ears. She looked like mouthwatering cotton candy. The light, spun confection that melted against his tongue had always been his favorite part of the fair. It was one of his secret weaknesses. It looked like Jenna was turning out to be another.

"There are two ways to look at it," she said, pulling on gloves. "I suppose you could think of it as an insult to your manhood. Personally, I think it'd take a man who was very sure and confident in his own masculinity to walk down the street wearing pink, not caring what anyone thought."

Logan nodded. "Excellent point. However, since I'm here on business, I do care what people think."

"Oh, yeah." She shook her head as if suddenly recalling a salient fact. "That buying the town bit. Sure." He automatically took a step forward and held her coat for her as she put it on. She glanced over her shoulder at him, no small hint of surprise and appreciation in her eyes. "Why, thank you."

"You're welcome." Good manners had been taught right after stoicism in the Jeffries household. His father had hammered home the one and his mother had been in charge of the other.

Jenna buttoned up and offered him another of those sunny grins. Damn, he could bask in her smile all day long. "All right, then, come on and meet Good Riddance. You're going to love it here."

She really didn't get it. It was on the tip of his tongue to point out that loving it, or even liking it, was immaterial. He just wanted to buy it and offer everyone a better life with the money they'd make. And not that it mattered, but somewhere inside, he knew that would disappoint Jenna. And he found, rather surprisingly, that he was loath to do that just yet. She'd come around to his way of thinking before all was said and done.

So, he nodded. "I'm sure I will."

LOGAN MUST SERIOUSLY BE on another planet if he thought he could buy the town, but he was cute in his earnestness. No worries. He'd get it soon enough. And Jenna really liked the way he held her coat and the door. She tamped back the inkling of disappointment that he hadn't actually come to see her and then let it go, determined to live in the moment.

Jenna preceded him out onto the snow-covered sidewalk. "Thank you, kind sir," she said, feeling a little bit like a princess in one of the Disney movies she loved to watch. Mulan, Tangled and Beauty and the Beast were her three faves. She'd bought all of them on DVD.

"You're welcome. Jenna, when you're introducing me today, let's not mention the buyout until I've had a chance to talk to Mrs. Swenson first. You know, out of respect, since she's the founder and mayor."

She stopped on the sidewalk and he skidded to a stop beside her. "You haven't told Merrilee yet?"

He looked kind of funny. "Well, no."

"So, why'd you tell her you were here?"

"I didn't say exactly. We got off on a tangent when I asked her about you."

"What? So you haven't mentioned wanting to buy the town to Merrilee?" *That* had never occurred to her. Merrilee hadn't been too busy to tell her about Logan's plan—she was in the dark. It explained a lot, like why Logan still saw buying the town as a viable option and why Merrilee hadn't called her a second time. Jenna remembered Merrilee's teasing tone, Teddy looking through the window at Jenna and Logan in a near-kiss and suddenly, it all spelled misunderstanding.

"No. I was going to talk to her and then…things just got kind of off track."

"Oh, great. This is just great." It was one thing if she'd thought at first that Logan had come to see her. But now everyone would think it. She felt kind of ill.

"You've lost me."

"Now everyone will think you came for me."

"Is that such a bad thing?"

"It's embarrassing."

"Thanks." She could've sworn she saw a momentary hurt in his eyes. There was certainly no glimmer of a smile.

Good grief, men and their delicate egos. "I don't mean *you're* embarrassing. People will be all excited because I've got a new man in my life. Then, I'll be pitied because you're not the new man in my life. So, then it'll be like oh, he's just here to buy the town and not because he came to see Jenna."

"I'm frightened to say that I almost, not quite, but *almost,* followed that illogical reasoning."

She planted her hands on her hips and glared at him. "I could kill you." Except she really did want to kiss him, at least just once, just so she could actually know what it felt like. That mouth…

"No worries. If we keep standing out on the sidewalk to have this conversation, I'll freeze to death sooner than later."

"I thought you were a big macho man who didn't need my scarf or hat."

"I don't, honey——"

"Don't call me honey in that condescending tone." Not when she'd fantasized about hearing it for real.

"I don't, *Jenna,* as long as I'm moving to keep my blood flowing and not standing in one spot turning into a human popsicle while you fall apart because people might think I traveled all the way from Atlanta to Good Riddance because I couldn't stay away from you." He made it sound totally preposterous.

He started walking and she had a choice. She could either walk or stand there staring at his back. She walked because she wasn't done with him. "I swear. I thought you were supposed to be smart." He was the one who was preposterous. "It would be fine if you'd done that."

"It would've?" This time he stopped, looking at her as if she'd lost her mind.

"Of course. The problem is, it'll already be all over town. By now everyone thinks you came for me. But you didn't."

"So, the embarrassing part is that I'm not a home-town stalker?"

Humph. Didn't the man possess a romantic bone in his body? Apparently not. "FYI, that wouldn't make you a stalker."

"Oh, really? Then what would it make me, considering we never exchanged more than a couple of words in high school?"

How well she remembered those words. "Misguided, for sure, since you turned down the opportunity to escort me to Homecoming." It felt good to say that. The wind gusted down the street and she resumed walking, this time in the opposite direction. She was cold and she had on suitable clothing, but still, the wind cut through her coat. He must be freezing. Even annoyed with him, she couldn't help but feel concerned. They needed to get inside soon. "Oh…just never mind. But we're going to do some damage control right now."

"How's that?"

She grabbed his arm and pulled him out into the street, toward the bed and breakfast. "Before I introduce you to anyone, we're going to find Merrilee and set the record straight. It's already too late but the sooner we nip this in the bud, the better."

"By all means, if that'll make you happy." Snow frosted his hair and she wanted to reach up and sweep it off. She shoved her hand in her pocket instead.

Ridiculously, what would make her happy was if he said he'd come all this stinking way to see her, but that wasn't happening. "Happy's a stretch, but it'll do for now."

They walked in the front door of the bed and breakfast, Jenna closing the door behind them. Merrilee and Bull, in the airstrip office that was the back half of the building, looked up.

"Hey, Jenna," Bull said, enveloping her in a quick bear hug. Ever since she'd made the decision to stay last year, Bull and Merrilee had kind of adopted her. It wasn't as if she didn't have plenty of parents but it was nice to have a pair that weren't marrying and divorcing almost as frequently as they changed their underwear. "So, this is your friend, Logan? Nice to meet you."

"Pleased to meet you, as well."

While Bull shook his hand, Jenna shot Logan an I-told-you-so look. "Logan needs to talk to you guys," Jenna said.

Bull and Merrilee exchanged their own look. "Sure thing," Merrilee said. She peered closer at Jenna, "Are you upset, honey? In the year I've known you, I don't think I've ever seen you angry. Not even when you found out what a bottom-feeder Tad was."

Jenna forced a smile. "No. Logan just needs to set the record straight." She might've dragged him over here but she'd let him tell Merrilee—that was, after all, why he was here.

That earned her another questioning look from both Bull and Merrilee.

"Okeydokey, then. Why don't we sit over here?" Merrilee said moving to the sitting area in front of the television. Dwight had apparently left for the day, since both rockers near the woodstove sat empty.

Jenna peeled out of her coat, gloves, hat and scarf. The pot bellied stove kept the room nice and toasty.

"How about a cup of coffee first?" Jenna asked Logan. "You could probably use something to warm you up."

"Sure, but I'll get it." Logan moved toward the coffeepot. He was obviously a man comfortable with being in charge. He glanced back over his shoulder. "Anyone else?"

Everyone declined. Merrilee and Bull settled in the armchairs, which left Jenna to share the love seat with Logan. Jenna sat and traced the flower pattern on the brocade fabric of the loveseat's arm with her fingertip. She was pretty sure it was a peony.

Merrilee talked while Logan poured. "So, have you had a chance to see much of the town?"

Behind her, Jenna heard Logan's shoes sound on the wood floor until he got to the braided rug that defined the seating area.

"Only what I saw on the way to Jenna's and back here."

Jenna wasn't surprised that Bull sat silently, merely observing. He was a man of few words, which was just as well considering Merrilee was a woman of many. Bull didn't talk a lot, but when he did, people listened.

Logan sat next to Jenna, the cushions shifting with his weight. He was close enough that she could smell his aftershave and a primal longing swept through her. He sat farther on the cushion's edge, leaning forward, his forearms braced on his spread knees, holding the coffee cup between them. She noticed his hands were broad. Once again her pulse raced at his nearness, even though she was thoroughly, and as Merrilee had pointed out, very uncharacteristically, put out with him.

"I appreciate you taking the time to sit down with me," Logan said. "I do know Jenna from back home. We went to high school together and it's great to see her again. But reconnecting with her..." Was that what they were doing, reconnecting? "...is just a side benefit to my trip." Jenna hoped she managed not to wince because it stung to hear herself referred to as a side benefit, although anything more would've just been foolishness she supposed. She didn't miss Merrilee's glance her way. "I'm with Jeffries Mining Consolidated—"

A look passed between Merrilee and Bull before she cut Logan off. "You're here about the gold?" A faint frown creased her brow. "I could've sworn..." she said under her breath, as if musing aloud. She shook her head and put on a smile. "So, what can we do for you?"

His face, turned toward Merrilee, offered Jenna a side view of the faint frown that wrinkled his forehead. "You are obviously aware of the gold."

Merrilee's laugh wasn't unkind. "Of course we are." She smiled, shaking her head. "We're not rubes, you know. Billy Sisnuket, he's the local shaman, told me all about it when I decided to build a town here."

"He told you about it twenty years ago?"

"Sure did. We are sitting smack dab on top of a gold mine. Isn't that cool?"

Jenna noticed Logan hadn't touched the coffee at all, he'd simply held the mug cupped in his hands. He must've been freezing. It was also impossible not to notice how his hair teased at the back of his collar and the width of his shoulders.

"We do think it's pretty cool, which is why we'd like to buy the town." A smile curved Logan's mouth, or at least the half she could see. "Of course, we'll want to keep the airstrip and the restaurant." Jenna listened as he outlined meeting with property and business owners individually to work out details. He finished up his spiel and sat looking expectantly at Merrilee.

"Okay," she said, her hands folded in her lap.

"I believe your charter doesn't specify who can and can't sell property."

Jenna, along with everyone else in the room, knew that if he'd come to make an offer, he knew good and well what was and wasn't specified in that charter. It was a matter of public record and his company would've thoroughly researched it.

"No. I left where I was because I didn't want anyone telling me what I could or couldn't do. That's the way I set my town up."

Jenna smiled. Tad had no idea what he'd set in motion.

"I figured the whole 'do unto others' business was applicable," Merrilee continued. "We're set up as individuals but we do vote as a town on what kind of business is set up."

Yep, Jenna's spa had to be voted on by everyone and she'd been happier than a clam when it passed. She didn't think she'd realized just how much she wanted it until just before it had been approved. Sometimes it was scary to allow yourself to want something so much, she thought, glancing at Logan.

"Considering how popular brothels were at one time in these parts, we thought a town vote was important, although there's nothing wrong with a woman making a living if that's how she chooses to do it." She winked at Logan.

Logan smiled and leaned back, as if to show how relaxed and comfortable he was with the conversation. But Jenna could literally feel the tension inside him. "Everyone here will be able to retire in comfort after this," he said.

"Is that a fact? I'm sure that might appeal to folks in other parts. But I have to tell you, Mr. Jeffries, we've discussed the possibility and we're not selling." The subject had come up at a town meeting and the decision had been unanimous.

"I think once you take a look at the proposal,

you'll reconsider. It's very generous." He raised his cup to his lips and sipped. "Good coffee, by the way."

Merrilee nodded. "It comes off of a little ole island in the Hawaiian archipelago. I grind it fresh every day."

"Delicious." Jenna wanted to snicker at Logan's faintly bemused expression. Obviously, he wasn't going to take no for an answer. "As far as the airstrip and restaurant, we'd like to buy it from you then hire you and your husband to run it. That's a real win-win situation," he continued, as if he couldn't believe Merrilee's words.

Merrilee waved her hand in the air. "I haven't time to discuss it now. I've got to get back to work." She stood and Bull followed suit, leaving Logan no choice but to stand as well.

"I understand," he said. Reaching into his pocket, he pulled out an electronic gadget. "When would be a good time for us to schedule an appointment?"

"Don't you worry about an appointment. I'm always either here or there. You go out and acquaint yourself with everyone. Bull brought over a coat for you to borrow until your luggage arrives. You can't be running around out there like that." She patted him on the arm. "We don't want you getting sick."

Bull nodded toward the wall behind Merrilee's desk. "It's the brown jacket with the plaid lining hanging over there."

"Thanks. I appreciate the loaner."

"Anytime."

"Do you feel better?" Logan said, turning to Jenna while Merrilee and Bull crossed the room. "Are you still upset or are you okay to show me around?"

Jenna wasn't exactly sure how she felt. She needed a little time when he wasn't sitting right next to her to sort it out. She did know, however, that she didn't want to get up and walk away from him.

"Yes, I'll show you around. We'll check out the spa—"

"Which I'm fully prepared to buy."

She merely smiled and continued as if he hadn't spoken. "—another time. You might've eaten but I'm starving and there are always people to talk to at Gus's."

"Gus's sounds like an excellent place to start."

That's what Jenna thought, too. Logan was about to discover some things weren't for sale.

5

NELSON LOCKED THE CLINIC door behind him, stepping out into the enveloping darkness. He glanced in the direction of Gus's. He should go down and check out Jenna's friend. He'd also find some of the crew, Skye and Dalton, Clint and Tessa, Sven, Bull's nephew, Dirk, who'd arrived a month ago, and Teddy gathered for dinner and conversation. Or if they weren't there, they would be soon.

Instead, he turned away from where the light spilled out of Gus's, illuminating the white snow blanketing the ground. He needed to talk, but he didn't feel social. He would meet Jenna's friend tomorrow.

Besides, none of them would understand his dilemma, not even Jenna. She'd listen and she'd sympathize but she wouldn't truly get it. And he couldn't talk to anyone in his clan, it was too risky. He was tempted to confide in his cousin, Clint, but Clint wouldn't truly understand, either. Being half white and half native, Clint possessed a measure of freedom Nelson would never know.

He'd never felt so alone, so out of sync with himself. The crunch of icy snow beneath his feet seemed to echo in the evening's silence. In the distance a wolf howled. There was no answering howl. The wolf stood alone as well.

Nelson opened the door and climbed into his truck. Cranking it, he sat and waited for the engine to heat while he considered his next move. He did not want to go home to face the four walls of his cabin that seemed to hold no answers for him. So where was he to go?

Once his engine warmed, he started driving away from town, in the opposite direction of his village which lay beyond Good Riddance. He'd go to Mirror Lake, the thermal lake that never froze and was a year-round haven for the mighty eagle. Clint had received his message at Eagle Lake. The raven had brought its message to Nelson but many questions remained. Perhaps Nelson, too, would find clarity there tonight.

LOGAN WATCHED THE REST OF the room watch him and Jenna as she led him to a large empty table on the far side of the restaurant. There was certainly nothing subtle about the residents of Good Riddance.

"People will start showing up soon. We'll sit here

so you can see everyone as they come in," Jenna said. She nodded in the direction of the farthermost pool table. "Rooster McFie's always looking for someone to take on in a game of pool. I'll hold the table if you want to play."

It wasn't hard to see how the man had come by the name of Rooster with his shock of red hair, squinty eyes and bright red beard. "I'll pass."

"Joey and Jack wouldn't mind starting a fresh game of darts if you'd rather do that," she said.

"Really, I'm fine. All I want is to have a drink and take a look around." *And sit across from you.* He didn't add that bit but it was the truth. Jenna was like a magnet, pulling him closer, and the hell of it was, he didn't know why. Sure, she was pretty, but there were a lot of beautiful women in the world. But there had always been something about Jenna that had set her apart.

"Okay, then," she said with a slight shrug.

The waitress who'd served him at lunch, Teddy, came over to their table. "What can I get for you?" she asked with an easy smile and a knowing look at him and Jenna. Her glance, however, settled on him.

"Scotch. Neat, if you will."

"Sure thing." She turned to Jenna. "The regular?"

"That'd be great. Teddy, this is Logan Jeffries. Logan, Teddy Monroe. Teddy's moving to New York in a few months to pursue an acting career."

See, right there, one dream funded, Logan thought.

The waitress would have more than enough money to live in the Big Apple for a while. "Congratulations. New York will be quite a change." And that qualified as the understatement of the year.

"No kidding. But I'm more than ready for it." She eyed the two of them once again. "We're glad to have you here. I hear you're a friend of Jenna's."

Jenna was right. The news had made it all over the one-street town already. "I am. We went to high school together but—"

Jenna cut him off with a smile. "Logan's here to buy the town."

"Right," Teddy said, her look proclaiming she didn't believe it.

He opened his mouth to speak but once again, Jenna beat him to the punch.

"His family owns a mining company."

"Oh, yeah? Ah." Teddy snapped her fingers. "It must be the gold. All right, then. I'll be right back with your drinks." She turned on her heel.

"Hey, can I have some pretzels, too?" Jenna said.

He was used to people asking his advice and direction. He was not, however, used to being talked around as if he was invisible. Or worse, having someone speak for him as if he was incapable of stringing a sentence together. Nonetheless, he held his tongue and let the ladies chat. Soon enough Teddy would be quizzing him about the particulars of the buyout.

"What about carbs?" Teddy said, quizzing Jenna about the choice of snack instead.

"I'll work it off in Zumba. I'm starving."

"True enough. Be right back."

That was it?

First, Merrilee Swenson had played him like a Stradivarius. Obviously she was positioning herself as not being interested in order to secure top dollar. Apparently her strategy was to make him wait, even before he threw the initial offer out on the table. And now this waitress was taking the same tact. It stood to reason, she wasn't rolling in cash if she was waitressing. And she was about to move to one of the most expensive cities in the world, yet she'd totally blown him off. Obviously the entire town was in on the conspiracy. No worries, he had plenty of time and the company had plenty of money.

In the meantime, what the hell was Zumba? He quirked an eyebrow at Jenna. "Zumba?"

Jenna laughed. "It's a cardio-dance workout set to Latin music. We all get together a couple times a week at the community center and exercise. I guess you could call it our fitness club."

A few moments later, Teddy came back with their drinks. "Here you are. One Scotch neat and a side of water, just in case."

"Thanks."

"Pretzels," she said, depositing a basket between them, "and one white-wine spritzer."

Jenna snagged one of the pretzels. "Thanks. I was just explaining Zumba to Logan."

Teddy turned to him. "Oh, you should come. It's so much fun! It doesn't matter whether you get all the steps or not."

"I don't—"

"Really, you should at least try it," Teddy interjected. He wasn't sure if he'd ever complete a sentence again. "We have some guys that come regularly. Petey—"

"He's a prospector and Donna's boyfriend," Jenna added. "You met Donna on your way into Curl's."

"Tall?" Maybe if he limited himself to one word, he could get it all out.

"Right." Teddy nodded, grabbing the conversational reins again. "Anyway, you'd never guess it but Petey can flat out bust a move."

"I'm not much of a dancer," Logan said. He didn't think it came with the Jeffries genetic packaging.

"You might be and just don't know it. Jenna's a good teacher."

"Ah, you're the instructor?" Even if he were aiming to *bust a move* with Jenna, it wouldn't be in a community center with a roomful of people and Latin music blaring.

"More like the leader. I just stand in front of the class and give everyone someone to follow."

"Don't let her fool you. She's good. You should see her salsa and cha-cha."

Another one of those blushes climbed Jenna's neck and face and Logan couldn't help but tease her. "Well, maybe I'll have to stop by to check it out, strictly as an observer."

She laughed, shaking her head, a challenging look in her eye. "You show up, you've got to participate."

Not even to seal the town deal. He grinned. "Fortunately for my two left feet, I left my cha-cha shoes at home."

From across the room, a man called out, "Hey, Teddy, I'm parched over here."

"Hold your horses, Jack. I'm coming." Laughing, Teddy turned. "I'll check back with you guys in a few."

Logan realized with a start he'd been having fun. Chasing on the heels of that nugget of insight came the thought that he'd nearly forgotten what fun was actually like. It wasn't part of his daily routine. He wasn't sure if it had ever been.

He raised his glass in Jenna's direction in a mini-toast and she did the same. His gaze held hers for a fraction longer than he'd intended and the laughter in her eyes became something totally different, a wariness combined with attraction.

"Hey, sweetie," a big man with an equally big voice said, shattering the moment. Pulling out one of the empty chairs at their table, he made himself at home. "Sorry to interrupt." The blond giant's expression wasn't in the least contrite. "But we need to talk about what we're going to do in your bedroom."

Logan was pretty damn sure the guy was her builder, or else he was just into the tool-belt look. Still, there was something about the bear of a man that left Logan itching to knock the smug expression right off his face.

Jenna laughed, rolling her eyes. "Sure, Sven." The Nordic name fit perfectly. Sven looked like the proverbial Viking minus the horned helmet and armor. "I want you to meet a classmate from back home, Logan Jeffries. Logan, Sven Sorenson, the most awesome builder in these parts. He's doing a great job on my place."

Ah. Okay. That *was* the connection. Logan hadn't forgotten for a second that Jenna had told him earlier that there was no man in her life. Although he still found that difficult to believe.

"You must've just gotten in today," Sven said as they shook hands across the table. Logan noticed the other guy's easy smile didn't falter.

"This afternoon."

The other man nodded. "That explains a lot. Now I know why Jenna wouldn't even give us locals a fighting chance. And now I know why Ms. Diligent here didn't bop down to check on her new digs this afternoon."

So Jenna had kept all the men at arm's length? Interesting. He'd bet top dollar they'd been lined up from here to Anchorage. And now this Sven thought Logan was the reason she'd kept to herself? Logan noticed she avoided even glancing his way, keeping her attention focused on Sven.

"Don't be silly," she said.

"Uh-huh." Sven looked from Jenna to Logan and then back to Jenna. "I see the way the lay of the land."

"Maybe I wasn't interested in you because you're obnoxious," she said to her builder, who was obviously a friend as well as a business associate.

Sven looked at Logan. "And here I thought that was part of my charm. Damn if I can figure women out."

"I hear you," Logan said. The one across from him in particular. He revised his initial impression. Sven was okay.

Jenna rolled her eyes at the two of them. "Seriously, Sven, Logan's here because he wants to buy the town."

"Cool." Sven eyed him appraisingly and beneath the good-humored facade Logan glimpsed the businessman. "You must have some deep pockets there." Finally. "Do you want the spa finished if you're buying the town?"

Before Logan could answer Jenna jumped in. "See? He's obnoxious, just like I said. He doesn't even live here."

Sven looked at Logan, held up his hands and shrugged. "Yet."

Damn. He was the one person who'd shown any enthusiasm and the guy wasn't even a citizen.

"What's the problem with my bedroom?" Jenna said, sipping her drink.

Logan settled back in his chair while she and Sven discussed the construction snafu. Funny, he'd always been attracted to Jenna in high school but he had to admit, he'd also pegged her as something of an airhead. But now listening to her discuss the construction with Sven, Logan saw a competent businesswoman. It made him want to know more about her and what made her tick.

And that was all well and good. Just as Rome hadn't been built in a day, Good Riddance wasn't going to be bought out in one, or even two. He was going to have plenty of time to get to the bottom of his fascination for this woman before he wrapped up his business and headed home.

ELLIE LIGHTFOOT HEARD THE engine's hum in the distance. Surely no one else was coming out to Mirror Lake tonight. She glanced over her shoulder. A faint glow on the other side of the rise signaled headlights. Clearly someone *was* about to interrupt her solitude.

She considered getting out of the water but the warmth felt heavenly and she hadn't gotten her full swim in yet. She loved the juxtaposition between the warm water and the crisp cold of the fall evening air. A quarter moon sliced the star-littered sky.

Her tent was pitched on the other side of a boulder so it wouldn't be visible to whoever was coming and she'd just stay close to the lake's edge and tread water. Hopefully the intruder wouldn't stay long. In all the years she'd been coming to Mirror Lake for her winter swims, no one else had ever shown up. Still, she didn't feel any sense of threat

The engine died and a door slammed. Chugach, her malamute, raised his head. "It's okay, boy," Ellie said in a quiet undertone to the dog. Whoever it was came alone. Damn. Her jeep. Her visitor would've parked close to it and would know someone was here.

The instant he topped the rise leading to the lake, Ellie recognized Nelson Sisnuket. Ellie's breath caught in her throat, the way it did every time she saw Nelson. She had dated his cousin, Clint, for a period of time because both Clint's grandmother and her parents had pushed the relationship. However, it was Nelson who caught her eye. She'd admired him since she'd returned from getting her teaching degree at University of Alaska.

Nelson, however, didn't seem to realize she existed. To him, she was just another member of a neighboring clan. And now it didn't matter because she was Clint's former girlfriend. Their clans would take a dim view of her seeing Nelson, who had to be above reproach. As a shaman-in-training, he was held to a higher standard.

"Ellie?" Nelson called into the night. No doubt he'd recognized her vehicle.

"Over here."

He looked around. "Where?"

The moon cast a sliver of light across the lake. She swam into the lit swath. "Here."

"You're in the water? Are you okay?"

She laughed at the mix of concern and incredulity in his normally even cadence. "Yes, I'm in the water and I'm fine. It's lovely to be in the warm water on a cold night."

His quiet laugh echoed through the stillness as he crunched through the snow toward her. "Yeah, well what about when you get out?"

"It's a little brisk. But I have a tent and I dry off and get dressed in there."

It was really kind of weird to be in the water, naked, carrying on a conversation with him but she was simply glad they were talking. "What brings you out here?"

"Answers. I needed to think. This seemed like a good place to do it." He glanced away from her, toward the moon, throwing his handsome features into relief. Her heart beat faster.

"It is a good place to think." A boldness she'd never before possessed coursed through her. "And out here is even better." She moved her arms through the water, setting ripples flowing across the calm surface. "Come on in. The water's fine."

6

"YOU CAN PUT YOUR CLOTHES in the tent next to mine, if you'd like. I'll look the other way until you're in."

"Are you naked?" Nelson realized how stupid that sounded. He didn't see any swimsuit straps where the moonlight kissed her shoulders and he dealt with patients in various forms of undress all day long. Then again, he wasn't standing on the edge of a steaming lake talking to them.

"Of course. It's the only way to swim when it's this cold." She dutifully turned her back and Nelson was struck by the way her hair flowed into the water's surface, giving the illusion she was one with the lake.

Her dog, Chugach, regarded Nelson as he removed the leather strip holding his own hair in place. Unzipping the tent flap, he crawled in, rezipped and quickly undressed. The air settled cold against his skin.

Fast-forwarding his senses and mind to the water's warmth, he stepped out onto the snow-covered ground. A mere three steps later, he was in the water, the fluid warmth embracing him as he waded deeper.

"It drops off sharply at about four feet in."

"I'm there now," he said, as the water rose to his chest. "You can turn around." He slid all the way into the water, totally submerging himself and then resurfaced.

It was a remarkably sensuous experience.

"Doesn't it feel wonderful?" Ellie said. It was as if she'd read his mind.

"It does." The warm water was invigorating with the cold air. His breath's steam mingled with that rising from the lake's surface. He didn't think he'd ever been as aware of a woman as he was of Ellie now, cloaked in the intimacy of the steaming water, the night and the lake's isolation. "So, do you come here often?"

Wow, that sounded like a cheesy line out of a B-grade movie.

Her soft laughter seemed to flow across the water. "Often enough. There's never been anyone else here though, when I've come on a fall evening. I find I can think when I'm in the water. It harmonizes my spirit. When I leave, I am both energized and at peace."

"I can understand that. There is something about this place. Clint found the answers he needed here." God, he was wired to say all the wrong things tonight. Clint's message had been to dump Ellie for the woman he'd wound up marrying, Tessa. "Um, sorry about that. That was thoughtless of me."

Once again, her soft laugh rippled between them. "It's fine. Clint and I never belonged together."

Her response startled Nelson. All this time he'd assumed she was nursing a broken heart. "I'm surprised."

"My pride was perhaps a little wounded, but my heart wasn't even bruised."

Two things struck him. First, once again she seemed to have tapped into his thinking. Second, he believed her. There was no anger in her assertion that Clint had not left her with a wounded heart.

"That's good. Pride recovers much more quickly and easily than a heart."

"You speak as if you've had yours broken."

"Perhaps bruised, but not broken."

Unlike most women he knew, Ellie didn't pry. Instead, she silently treaded water, giving him room to bring his troubled energy and questions to the lake.

He realized he had one answer right before him. Hadn't he needed someone to talk to, someone who would understand his dilemma, his position? Ellie floated near him like some water gift from the spirits.

"Do you ever feel trapped?" he said, breaking the encompassing quiet.

There was no hesitation, no contemplation. She responded with a simple "Yes" in her quiet voice that flowed over him with the same soothing warmth as the water.

"How so?" he said.

"By tradition. Expectation. By the very culture that makes me who and what I am."

Nelson nodded. It was as if she'd reached into his core and felt the same things he felt.

"You feel trapped as well?" Ellie said. "Is it by the rules that come with being the next shaman?"

"Yes." He bowed his head in a mixture of guilt and shame. He had never spoken the words aloud or had them spoken to him. Instead they had beat inside him like a trapped bird, wearing out his inner spirit.

He started at the soft touch against his shoulder. Ellie rested her fingers against his skin, her touch soothing. "Nelson, it's okay. Do you want to talk about it?"

"I want to go to medical school." The words seemed to hang on the cold autumn air. It was the first time he'd given voice to them. "I'm good at what I do." He had trained a couple of years ago as a medical technician, preparing him to marry his people's traditions with that of the white man's medicine. But it left no room for him to pursue the white man's medicine in the role of a doctor, and that was very much what he wanted.

There was no need to explain any of his dilemma

to Ellie. She understood all the implications. He either forsook his culture and his people or his dreams.

"I'm sorry," she said.

He reached up and wrapped his fingers around hers where they still rested on his shoulder. He still had no answers but he felt immeasurably better. "And what of you, Ellie Lightfoot? How do you feel trapped? What is it you want that you cannot have?"

She lowered her eyes. "I can't talk about it now."

He reached out and tilted her chin up with his finger. "That's all right. When you are ready, I am here to listen."

Over the ridge a wolf howled. Within seconds there was an answering call. The wolf he'd heard earlier was no longer alone.

JENNA COULD BARELY MOVE. Luckily, crowds didn't freak her out because there'd been a constant flow of people around their table all evening. And it hadn't helped when Logan had ordered a round of drinks for the house, on him. Well, no doubt it was his expense account.

He could buy drinks all night but it didn't mean the town was going to sell out. Across the table, Clint Sisnuket, one of the best native guides in the state and Nelson's cousin, was discussing cross-country ski trails with Logan.

Speaking of Nelson, well, thinking of Nelson rather, she hadn't seen him all evening. Jenna glanced around the crowded room. Nope, he wasn't here, which was kind of unusual. Since Nelson worked for Skye Shanahan, Skye might know where he was. Jenna was about to ask Skye, who was sitting across the table between Clint and her husband, Dalton, when Clyde Weaver walked up.

"I wanted to get a look at the feller that did the rest of us in," Clyde said, his thumbs hooked into the suspenders holding up his jeans. Standing as wide as he was tall, Clyde always reminded Jenna of a garden gnome.

"He's here to buy the town," Jenna said. Maybe she'd just make a flashcard to hold up. God knows, she'd uttered that phrase at least one hundred times within a two-hour period.

"So he says. Everybody knows Good Riddance isn't for sale." Clyde eyed Logan the same way Jenna checked out cuticles. He nodded. "He's the reason the rest of us haven't stood a chance with you. Granted, some of us are a little long in the tooth—" Clyde was probably pushing his late fifties "—but you haven't even gone for any of the young fellas. Now we know why."

It was like beating her head against a brick wall. Everyone was going to think what they wanted to anyway. "Now you know why."

And actually, she realized, there wasn't a man in Good Riddance, or anywhere else for that matter, that interested her as much as Logan did. It was as if whatever she'd felt for him at seventeen had been tucked away inside her, only to return now, bigger and more intense. She felt something for him, something she'd never felt before for any man.

Clyde looked over to the back corner of the room, caught Rooster's eye and held up four fingers. Rooster had opted out of pool in order to take wagers. He'd been busy all night in the back corner. Jenna had seen the flash of cash. A part of her was curious as to the exact nature of the bets but really, ignorance was bliss. However, Clyde had just wagered forty bucks.

"Say, what's with the broad in the green sweater playing poker?" Clyde said.

Broad in the green sweater? It took Jenna a second to realize he was referring to Norris, two tables over playing five card draw with Sven and his crew. She almost always beat the pants off of them. Jenna gave Clyde the rundown on Norris.

"You don't say? Well, where have I been?" Clyde said, smoothing his hand over the top of his hair, as if that would make a difference. It didn't but Jenna supposed he got credit for trying. "I might try my luck there," he said. "I like a woman with a little seasoning to her. Plus I've been working on some poems. Maybe she could give them a read and tell me what she thinks."

Clyde was a poet? Clyde and Norris together?

Who knew? Maybe. Love came in all shapes and sizes.

"Good luck."

Clyde, intent evident in his eyes, started in the direction of the card game. "Uh, Clyde," Jenna said.

"Yeah?"

"I wouldn't interrupt her during the game."

"I suppose you're right. Good point. Maybe I'll go hang out at the bar and compose an ode to her on a napkin."

"I think that's a better plan."

She smiled. Then just as it had been all night, her gaze was drawn to Logan. He'd been sitting across from her and he'd been swamped with people all evening, but time and again she'd glanced at him only to find him looking at her. And more than once, when she'd been talking to someone else, she'd felt his eyes on her.

She liked everyone in Good Riddance but suddenly, the noise and crowd were too much. It had been a long day and Jenna realized she was about five minutes away from being in the same state as a perm gone wrong—overprocessed. She needed to go home to her quiet cabin and have some time alone, just her and Tama.

"I'll see everyone tomorrow. I'm heading out," she said to the table in general.

Logan immediately spoke up, interrupting his

conversation with Clint. "Give me a second and I'll walk you home."

What? She'd managed to look after herself very well up to this point. Now Logan shows up and turns her world topsy-turvy and she's supposed to wait? She didn't think so. He hadn't come all this way to find her and she certainly hadn't just been sitting around waiting on him to show up. She had a full, complete life right here. And she'd done as she'd promised—she'd introduced him around.

"You don't have to walk me home." Their table grew quiet. "I'm perfectly capable of getting there by myself." Come to think of it, the entire room had grown quiet. She didn't care. Her gaze didn't falter. Neither did his. "In fact, I do that on a regular basis. This is Good Riddance. It's perfectly safe here."

"Jenna, I know I don't *have* to walk you home. I *want* to walk you home. And I'm going to, one way or the other. You escorted me here, I'm escorting you home."

"If you do that then everyone's really going to think there's something between us."

"Apparently they're going to think that regardless."

She simply couldn't help herself. "I told you so."

"Yes, you did, didn't you?" He looked cool as a cucumber sitting across the table, the entire restaurant watching them like spectators watching a tennis match. "So, may I walk you home or do I have to follow five paces behind like a stalker?"

She narrowed her eyes at him. If he thought he was going to throw her off course any more than he already had, he could think again. "I think I might like that."

"Walking with you or following five paces behind?"

"I suppose you might as walk with me. People are going to talk."

"They will regardless." He pushed his chair back, standing. "And now if you'll excuse us," he said to the room at large, "as you all just heard, the lady is ready to go home."

The room erupted, Rooster's back corner in particular. Logan and Jenna didn't exchange a word to each other as they made their way to the door. Logan held Jenna's coat for her and her whole body hummed at his mere nearness. This was precisely why she needed to be alone. She'd been in hyper-awareness mode from the second he'd been outside her door. He shrugged into his loaner jacket.

"See," said a woman at the table near the door. "That's what a gentleman's supposed to do for a lady."

Jenna and Logan stepped out into the star-sprinkled night, the sickle of a moon hanging as if suspended by a thread. Jenna welcomed the refreshing chill.

In silence, they walked along the sidewalk, the only sounds the crunch of snow underfoot and the faint sigh of the wind through the trees.

Caught up in her overwhelming awareness of him, she wasn't as careful of her footing as she usually was. She hit an icy patch on the sidewalk and slipped.

His reflexes quick, Logan caught her, steadying her, righting her against him. Her words of thanks faltered, buried by the avalanche of want that had been with her all day—the need to know his kiss, just once.

She leaned up, he leaned down and finally... At first his lips, like hers, were stiff with cold but within seconds they grew warm. Very warm. With a muffled groan, he pulled her closer, kissing her harder, deeper. It was sweet and hot and he tasted faintly of whiskey.

Jenna sighed and leaned into him, returning his kiss with all the passion that had been bottled inside her, simply waiting for the right man to release. She felt as if fireworks were going off in her.

They broke apart, the sound of their breathing seemed to fill the night. Wordlessly, they resumed walking. Logan, however, kept one arm wrapped around her waist. Jenna liked the weight of it, the steadiness it offered.

They had just passed Bull's hardware store when Logan broke the silence. "Why did you ask me to escort you to Homecoming all those years ago?"

The question seemed random but it really didn't surprise her. In the scheme of surprises, it was nothing compared to the fact that he'd actually turned up here today. And she'd gotten her comment in about his rejection earlier. Obviously neither of them had forgotten that incident twelve years ago.

But what did he mean, why had she asked him? That was crazy. "Why does anyone ask another person out? Because I wanted to go with you."

"You really wanted me to take you?" He turned his head to look at her, even though the night was fairly dark.

What the heck? "I asked you, didn't I? And we both clearly remember you said no."

"You seriously wanted me to go?"

"How many drinks did you have tonight?" Logan wasn't weaving or bobbing and he didn't sound incoherent, but he certainly wasn't making any sense.

"I'm sober. I'm just… Do you know why I turned you down?"

Stick a fork in her. She was nearly done. It had been an emotional roller coaster of a day. "Look, Logan. It hurt my feelings at the time—I'm not crazy about rejection—so if it's something awful, I'd rather you just kept it to yourself. I figured you turned me down because you didn't like me. Plain and simple."

"I turned you down because I thought you were asking me on a dare."

"You thought I'd actually do something like that?"

She couldn't have hid the hurt in her voice even if she tried. She didn't try. She stepped to the left, away from his arm. He had the good sense not to try to stop her. "Wow. I'd have preferred that you refused because you didn't like me."

"I didn't know you, Jenna. You were pretty and popular and I saw your friend waiting over at the water fountain…"

"You thought I was one of those mean girls." She was incredulous. "Really? Where did you ever get an idea like that? As corny as it sounds, I've always tried to treat people the way I want to be treated. For the most part, it's worked out well."

"I didn't know." He spoke quietly, a wealth of regret in his voice.

The way she saw it, she had two choices. She could get all hurt and clam up and let him go on his merry way, none the wiser as to what had actually happened on her end. Or…she could be honest. "Bethany was there for moral support. It took me two weeks to work up the nerve to ask you."

"It did?"

"I went home and cried afterward." She had to admit she hoped he felt bad about that.

"Oh, God, I'm sorry." He did. *Good*.

"I had such a thing for you."

"You had a thing for me?"

What the heck? She'd just put it all out there. "Okay. Let's just lay this out one time and be done with it. I had a terrible crush on you. I thought you were smart and good-looking and you seemed kind of nice even if you were aloof, but I liked that." They turned to walk up to her front door. The porch light seemed very bright after the dark walk over. "I screwed up my courage and asked you to escort me. You turned me down because you thought I was the type of girl who would prank someone and then laugh at them." They climbed the two stairs to the front porch. "End of story."

He ran his hand over his head. "I was an idiot."

"You won't get any argument from me." Tama peered at her through the window from inside the house. He was probably ready for his dinner. "Well, we're here. Good night."

"I could come in."

She shook her head. "No. I'm tired. I need some time alone."

"Okay." He raised his hand as if to touch her face and then seemed to think better of it. He put his hand in his pocket. "Can I see you tomorrow?"

"You know where I work and have a good idea just how big the town is. It would be more difficult for you to avoid me than to see me tomorrow."

"You're not going to make this easy, are you?" No, she wasn't. "What I'm asking is, would you like to go out with me tomorrow night? I'm talking about a date."

Was he only asking because he thought it would

help his cause? She supposed she was as suspicious of his motives now as he'd been of hers back then. "It's not going to make any difference in your chances of buying the town."

"It's not about me buying the town."

She wanted to believe him. She wanted it so badly, she was afraid to let herself think it. But if she'd laid it on the line, so could he. "Then what's it about?"

"Why does one person ask another person out?" He was echoing her own words back to her. "Because they want to spend time with them."

It was crazy how happy his words made her. "Okay."

"Okay, as in yes?

"Yes," she said.

"Six? Here?"

"That's fine. What are we doing? I need to know what to wear."

"I don't know yet." He didn't exactly smile but his eyes did. "Dress warm. Layer."

He leaned down and pressed a sweet, safe kiss to her lips, that nonetheless set her heart pounding. His fingers lingered against her cheek for a moment. "Good night."

He turned and walked down the stairs, the dark swallowing him.

Jenna opened the door and stepped inside, closing it behind her. Tama greeted her, rubbing against her legs, loudly announcing it was his dinner time.

"I know. Give me a second or two."

She leaned back against the door, her lips still tingling from his kiss, her legs slightly unsteady. She had a lot to sort through in her head, but there was one undeniable fact that didn't need any sorting.

She was crazy about that man.

7

"I HAVE TO GET HOME," Ellie said. "My parents will be worried about me if I'm gone much longer."

"I don't want you to go." Nelson hadn't planned to say it but the words spilled from inside him. Ellie looked startled. "I mean, I've enjoyed your company."

Her smile seemed to move through him. "I've enjoyed your company, too. When I first heard your truck coming, I was annoyed. I wanted whoever it was to simply leave quickly. No one else has ever been here when I was here like this, but I'm glad you came. And I'm glad it was you."

Her words wrapped around him like a warm blanket on a cold night.

"Me, too."

She nodded. "I need to change in the tent. Will you please turn your back while I get out or would you rather get out first?"

"No. You go first." He turned to face the lake's opposite shore. "Go ahead and get out."

The water rippled as she exited the lake and he heard the zipper.

"Thanks. You can turn back around now," she said from inside the tent.

He settled back in the water, highly aware that just a few feet from him, Ellie was naked and drying off in the tent. Even though he spent his days among patients in various states of undress, it was arousing and enticing to know Ellie, with her lean golden body, was toweling herself dry just a few feet away.

For the first time in a long time, Nelson felt sexual desire. He hadn't found anyone who awakened that side of him in years, but now, with the warm water lapping at him and images of Ellie dancing in his head, his sexuality was reawakening.

He'd seen her in a new light tonight. She'd looked like a water goddess with her hair streaming over her bare shoulders, the moonlight burnishing her skin to gold.

He heard her rustling in the tent. Her dog sat guard, waiting, watching Nelson. In a few minutes she unzipped the flap and emerged, her hair hanging down her back in a single plait.

"There's an extra towel. I always bring one in case of an emergency. Your turn." She presented her back, affording him privacy. The air felt bracingly frigid as he emerged from the warm lake. That certainly took care of his arousal.

Kneeling in the tent, Nelson dried off using the folded towel. Her scent seemed to hang in the air, a fresh clean smell of the woman herself, not lotions or perfume. Nelson pulled on his dry clothes and tied his hair back. His socks and boots went on last.

Ellie stood waiting, a serene smile on her face. How had he overlooked her beauty all this time? It was as if scales had fallen from his eyes.

"Do you need help getting everything packed up?"

"Thanks but I've got a system." She knelt and leaned into the tent, gathering the wet towels and placing them in a bag. Within a couple of minutes she'd efficiently packed the tent away also. "Okay, so that's it."

Walking side by side, the dog trotting ahead, they made their way back to their respective vehicles.

Nelson stopped by her jeep and waited while she stored her tent in the back. "So, will you be here tomorrow night?"

"No. But I will the night after tomorrow."

"Would you mind if I returned?"

"I'd like that." She opened her driver's door. "I'll be here around the same time."

"I'll see you then."

He stepped away so she could close her door. He made his way to his truck, feeling better than he'd felt in a long time.

He whistled under his breath. Perhaps he didn't have the answers he'd sought, but his spirit felt lighter. After all, he had a date with a beautiful woman in two days time.

THE NEXT MORNING, LOGAN wrapped up the last of his emails and logged off. He'd accomplished in two hours what would've taken all morning in the office. It was business as usual back in Atlanta. No surprises. No, everything that had shaken up his very routine life was right here. And she had a name. Jenna.

He poured a second cup of coffee from the in-room coffeemaker. With business out of the way, he allowed himself to think about last night. Actually, that was a joke. Jenna had been on his mind the entire time he'd been working. Usually he was good at compartmentalizing, but dammit, the woman wouldn't stay out of his head.

He was still amazed that she'd had a thing for him back when they'd been kids. And, like a coward, he hadn't admitted he'd had his own thing for her at the time. He, however hoped he'd rectify that mistake sometime today. Either in words—or in action.

More importantly, he knew there was definitely something between them now. He'd gone to sleep with her taste on his lips. He ached for her, longed for her with an intensity unlike anything he'd ever known before. She'd tasted like everything good in life.

Carrying his coffee cup, he crossed to the window overlooking Main Street. Headlights illuminated the white snow in the street and a team of sled dogs, locked into their traces, pulled a sled down the road the musher standing on the back traces encouraging them.

A pickup pulled to the front of the dry goods store. A bundled figure moved along the opposite sidewalk. Even without the bright pink hat and scarf, he would've recognized Jenna anywhere. He'd realized yesterday that a part of him still remembered the way she moved, her gait, the bounce in her step. Time hadn't changed that and he'd never forgotten.

She paused and looked up. While it wasn't as dark as last night, the town seemed to be wrapped in a twilight, dawn not quite emerging yet. As unlikely and as irrational as it seemed, he could've sworn her gaze scanned the distance and locked with his.

Desire shook him to the center of his being. It had been a long time since he'd wanted a woman the way he wanted her. Actually, the last time he'd wanted a woman this badly had been years ago…and it had still been Jenna. In the past twelve years, there hadn't been anyone else who affected him the way she did.

She looked away and resumed walking. He found himself counting the hours until he could show up on her doorstep again. And then what? He knew all the businesses in town. Gus's was the only restaurant. It was also the only bar. There was no movie theatre. No museum. As far as date options went, well, there weren't many.

He heard the plane before he saw it. If everything was back on plan, his luggage should be onboard. And today he'd work at getting Merrilee onboard with the buyout. He'd known from the preliminary report that she was the key. If he persuaded her, everyone else in town would follow suit. But first he needed to get the proposal in front of her.

He headed downstairs, reaching the bottom stair at the same time Dalton came in the back door, Logan's luggage in hand.

Dalton grinned at him. "Now that's what I call timing."

"I heard your plane coming in," Logan said with a smile.

"Here you go. I'm sure it'll be nice to change duds."

"Thanks." Logan grabbed the suitcase in his left hand and shook Dalton's hand with his right. "I appreciate it."

"All in a day's work. Speaking of work…" Dalton turned to Merrilee. "I'm going to run a motor part over to Donna." He headed for the door.

"The coffee'll be here," Merrilee called after him. She offered Logan a smile. "Good morning." She nodded toward his suitcase. "Looks like your day just got a whole lot better."

"That it did."

"Unless you're in a hurry, be sure to grab a cup of coffee and a cinnamon roll or two." They did smell damn good. "Lucky made them this morning. They're not as good as Gus's but since Gus isn't here…" She turned her attention to the old man sitting in the rocking chair. "You want a cinnamon roll, Dwight?" she shouted. She glanced at Logan, "He's mostly deaf."

He'd learned last night, while hanging out at Gus's, that the actual Gus was a Paris-trained chef named Augustina who'd taken refuge from a sadistic former fiancé in Good Riddance. Gus had returned to Manhattan but she and her new fiancé, not the sadistic stalker, were returning in December to get married. Gus sounded like quite a character, but then everyone in Good Riddance seemed to be one. Between Christmas, the Chrismoose festival, which he'd heard about from several people and the upcoming wedding, the place would be hopping in a couple of months. For such a tiny little town, it was amazing how much activity there was.

He placed his suitcase next to the stairs and poured another cup of coffee. Then he grabbed a cinnamon roll.

"Just go ahead and take two. They're that good," Merrilee said.

Suddenly hungry, he snagged another one and sat in the empty chair by her desk.

"I'm sure it was nice to see Jenna again after all this time," Merrilee probed as he bit into the pastry. Butter, cinnamon, sugar and a plump juicy raisin combined with the fresh, yeasty roll was incredible. If Gus's was actually better... He finished chewing and swallowed.

"Good, huh?"

"I'm glad I wasn't here for Gus's. And yes, it was good to see Jenna." He took another bite, thinking. Desperate times called for desperate measures. "I could really use some advice, if you've got a minute. I asked Jenna out tonight but I don't know where to go."

"Is this a date?" Merrilee asked, a teasing glint in her eyes.

Logan felt like the luckiest guy in the world. Damn. He had a date with Jenna Rathburne. Finally. He knew he was grinning like a fool and quite frankly, he didn't care. "Yes, it sure is."

Merrilee tapped her pencil against her desk blotter. "Dating can be something of a challenge in Good Riddance. You're sort of limited." That was an understatement. "You have to be resourceful. And creative."

He was so out of luck. "I'm a numbers kind of guy. Asking you for advice is the extent of my resourcefulness and creativity. But I want to make it really special. I sort of screwed something up—no, not sort of, I *did* screw up in a big way—and I'd like to make it up to her by doing something special."

Merrilee laughed. "Let's see. Karaoke isn't until tomorrow night. Skye Shanahan's teaching a CPR certification course over at the community center tonight but I don't think that's what you'd want to do on a date."

"Not particularly."

Merrilee brightened, snapping her fingers. "I've got it. You could always go on a picnic."

Obviously it took a different breed of person to live out in the Alaskan bush. He didn't want to come across as a wuss but... "I think I'm missing something. It's not going to get above freezing today, much less tonight."

"Innovation, Logan, innovation. I've got a basket tucked away somewhere. We'll set you up with a blanket, a few candles and dinner from Gus's. You and Jenna can have a picnic right there in her cabin."

"That sounds good, but it will be obvious I didn't come up with the idea on my own."

"She won't care whether you came up with it yourself. Not when you show up on her doorstep packing a romantic candlelight picnic. Trust me on this. I'm a woman."

Merrilee knew Jenna and if she said that's what he should do, then that's what he intended to do. "I take it I can get the candles at the dry goods store?"

"Absolutely. While you're there, you can nose around and see if there's anything else that might strike your fancy. Teddy'll help you pull together the food."

There was still one thing that wasn't making any sense. "Why would the two of you go to all of that trouble?"

"Why did you come here, Logan?"

"Well, as I explained yesterday—"

She waved her hand. "I know your company wants to buy us out. I've been waiting for someone to show up ever since your man scouted us out in July. But why you? This isn't in your normal job description. For goodness sake, you're the CFO. I checked out the company website. Why are you here instead of Mr. Fishcher?"

"I was due a vacation and I've always wanted some time in Alaska—"

"Logan, you've got the money to come up here any time you wanted to. Why didn't you come in the summer when the days are long and there are a lot more interesting things to do?"

"This way, I was killing two birds with one stone. My company wants to make a deal and I wanted to look Jenna up."

Merrilee's gaze was shrewd. "She was sitting in your backyard for eleven years. Have you ever stopped to wonder why you waited until there was another country between the two of you?"

Damn. He hadn't thought about it at all but the way she put it made him sound less than logical. "No. I...well..."

"It's okay. You'll figure it out." The phone rang. "Excuse me." She answered. "Uh-huh. Today? We were just there this morning. It's not scheduled until tomorrow. What? They want today? Right." Her smile couldn't possibly get any bigger. "Fine. We'll be there today, right after lunch. Yep, the going rate for a round-trip flight. Okay. Got it covered." She hung up. "That's a class act."

"Was that the florist?"

"Uh-huh. You know that's a pretty steep delivery fee you're paying there. You could have saved yourself a ton of money waiting a day."

"No, it's already been too long."

"Good enough then. We'll get the flowers you ordered here today. And not that it matters, but did you come up with that idea on your own?"

"I did."

She patted his arm. "That beats a picnic any day, hon. The two things together...well, you did good." She settled back in her chair. "Now that we've talked about matters of the heart, let's discuss business."

Logan instantly switched gears. "Absolutely. I'm ready."

Merrilee made the shift seamlessly as well. "Let me save you some time and aggravation. Quite simply, Good Riddance is not for sale. It doesn't matter what you're offering, it doesn't matter where you propose we relocate, the buyout isn't going to happen."

"Would you at least take a look at the proposal?"

"Of course. Then you can say you gave it your best shot."

"I don't understand how you can turn down an offer when you don't even know what it is."

"There are two types of people in life, Logan. There are those who are convinced the grass is always greener on the other side. Then you've got others who know that whatever's on the other side can't possibly compare with how great things are now. Each and every one of us has our own trials and tribulations. I'm not going to pretend we've found paradise, but what we have found is darn close.

"We're a community of people who care about one another, who look out for one another, and who respect one another. From the very second I parked my motor home on what was mostly a dirt track at the time, I knew this was a special place. Our motto—*where you get to leave behind what ails you*—is right on the money. I stopped, I parked, I got out and it was as if my heart found the balm it needed. And that, my friend, is something cash can't buy. I know you think we were all holding out to drive the price up. Not a bit. We've had this discussion numerous times over the years and the outcome has always remained the same. Price isn't a factor.

"So, I hope you'll kick back and relax and take the vacation you say you've needed before you move on to the next location on your list."

"And if I tell you I intend to fly out tomorrow?"

She shrugged, amusement in her blue eyes. "Then we'll book your flight for tomorrow. Is that what you want to do?"

"No. I'll finish out my vacation here. And I'll leave the proposal with you, although I believe you when you say the town's not for sale. I'm a businessman. I know when to cut my losses." He stood. "I'll drop the proposal off on my way out, just so you can see what you'll be missing out on. It'll make me feel better." He shook her hand. "It's been a pleasure doing business."

"Likewise. Now let your hair down and enjoy our little town as much as we do."

The front door opened and a woman he recognized from last night barreled in.

"Morning, Norris," Merrilee said.

Norris. That was her name. Logan knew it was something a little unusual.

"Morning, Merrilee." She nodded in Logan's direction. "Morning, Jeffries." She plopped a stack of folded papers onto the desk. "Hot off the presses. The first edition of The Good Riddance Observer." She pulled one off the top and handed it to him. "Your girl is our feature story."

It was on the tip of his tongue to deny she was

his girl, but then he thought better of it. For now, it seemed that she just might be. "So I see."

Jenna, her smile bright and generous, stood holding her cat in black and white on the front page. "I'm looking forward to reading it." And he was.

"Say, I'd like to snag an interview with you while you're here, if you wouldn't mind. You know, a story on chasing the pot of proverbial gold, a twenty-first century prospector."

Funny, he'd never thought of it that way. He bet Jebediah would like the analogy. "I believe I'm going to have some free time. Sure."

"Good deal. How about lunch today? Gus's at one?" He nodded as she was still talking, all the while heading toward the door. "Gotta run. Our feature story is doing my nails and then I've got a date with a younger man."

"Do tell," Merrilee said as Norris opened the front door.

"Clyde. I promised to help him with his poker game. You know there aren't a lot of dating options here."

Merrilee winked at Logan. "Innovation. Innovation."

JENNA WALKED ALONG THE sidewalk, enjoying the sun on her way back from checking in on the spa, which was coming along beautifully. Tama trotted along beside her.

It was all she could do not to dance along the sidewalk. She had a date tonight. And it wasn't just any date. She had a date with Logan, who was a better kisser than she'd even imagined. Now she wanted to know if he did everything better than he did in her head.

And quite frankly that posed a dilemma.

She wanted Logan Jeffries in the carnal sense. There was no doubt about it, he was just what she'd been looking for all this time. With every fiber of her virginal being, she wanted that man inside her, on top of her, behind her, beneath her. As far as she was concerned, they had a whole lot of ground to cover. But—why did life have to hand you "buts"?— she'd read a million times in magazines and books that a woman shouldn't sleep with a man on a first date because then he'd think she was promiscuous and lose interest. But Logan was only going to be in town for a limited amount of time. If she waited until tomorrow night, she'd only have two nights left.

A horn blew and she waved without really looking, wrapped up in her thoughts. The irony of it hit her. She was a twenty-nine-year-old virgin, worried Logan might think she was easy for sleeping with him on their first date. How crazy was that?

Her cell phone rang in her pocket. She pulled it out and saw Merrilee's number. "Hey."

"Where are you?"

Jenna laughed. "On my way back from the spa. Where are you?"

"Sitting at Curl's, waiting on you."

She'd been floating on Cloud Nine all day—had she forgotten an appointment? "Did I have you down in my book?"

"No. You had a package arrive on a flight this afternoon and I thought I'd walk it down."

"Okay. I'm almost there." She'd ordered some darker nail colors for the winter but she hadn't expected them to arrive this soon.

She opened the door and walked in. Merrilee was sitting in the barber shop chair looking like the cat who'd just swallowed the canary.

"You're looking pretty pleased with yourself," Jenna said, smiling as well.

Merrilee smirked—there was no other word for it—it was a flat-out *smirk*. "Special delivery for Ms. Jenna Rathburne in Good Riddance, Alaska," she said, pointing to the manicure table behind Jenna.

Jenna turned. Her mouth dropped open and she leaned against the door, speechless. A dozen long-stemmed yellow roses were interspersed with baby's breath in a crystal vase. They were stunningly, breathtakingly beautiful.

"Oh, honey, don't cry."

She hadn't even realized she *was* crying. "They're they…you're sure they're for me?"

"You are Jenna Rathburne, aren't you?"

"No one's ever... Logan?"

Merrilee shrugged, grinning from ear to ear. "I didn't read the card, hon. I just delivered them."

"But there's no florist in town."

"Juliette picked them up. I told you, sweetie, they're special delivery."

Her hand was shaking so hard, she could barely hold the envelope. She pulled out the card. *I should've said yes. Please forgive me.*

That was it. Her legs were no longer capable of holding her. Jenna sank into her chair. "Merrilee, I..."

"He did good. You know he paid the round trip fare to have them picked up and delivered today."

"I am so going to sleep with him tonight."

"What?" Merrilee asked, laughing.

Jenna explained her dilemma. "But the flowers, the card... I don't want to wait any longer, Merrilee."

"Jenna, the way I see it, the two of you have been waiting twelve stinking years. I say go for it."

"It's a little bit like deciding to have sex in a gold-fish bowl."

"Well, that sort of comes with the territory when you live up here. So you might as well just relax and enjoy it. Heck, everyone's going to think you did, whether you do or not."

"True enough. And if everyone wasn't talking already, these flowers will seal the deal." She drew a deep breath. "Do you have any idea where I can get a condom?"

Merrilee laughed. "I can hook you up with protections. Not that Bull and I need it at our age—I mean we are sexually active but I hit menopause a couple of years ago. Even though I wasn't really looking forward to the hot flashes and all that business, it hasn't been bad and I'll have to say not having a period is downright nice. But I keep a supply on hand, right along with any other toiletries my guests might need. But you're going to need more than one. How about half a dozen?"

Jenna swallowed hard. "Six? That seems like a lot."

"You're better off having a few extras than running short. He's young and he strikes me as virile. You know how that can go."

"Um, well, the problem is I don't know."

"I'm feeling you there. I do distinctly recall Tad being a one-hit wonder and that was only when the stars were aligned just right. Then again, I should quit being such a crank. It was a long time ago and it's tacky to kiss and tell."

"He said you were frigid." She'd never told Merrilee that before because there just hadn't been any point. But she didn't want Merrilee to feel bad about saying anything about Tad now. He deserved anything she wanted to say about him.

"Impotent little-dick bastard. Sorry."

"No apologies necessary. I'm just as glad I skipped that."

"You mean you never, you and Tad, didn't...?"

Jenna shook her head. "I was never feeling it."

"Lord, honey, I was married to the man and I wasn't feeling it, either—that's cause it was hard to find. I definitely upgraded with Bull. How do you think he got that nickname?"

"I always assumed it's because he's built like a bull."

"Trust me, honey, he is, in every respect." Merrilee took a moment to fan herself. "But let's get back to what we were talking about."

"Well, I've never really wanted it with anyone, but I think Logan might be the one, so..."

"Are you saying you've never, not with anyone?"

"Never. No one."

"Well, I'll be damned. Were you wanting to wait until you were married?"

"No, and I sure don't think I'm going to marry Logan. I just wanted some kind of connection on my part. I'm not talking about love, I'm talking about passion."

"Lots of women confuse the two."

"Tell me about it. My mother tops the list." And while Jenna loved her mother, she didn't want to relive her mother's mistakes.

"You must be as nervous as a cat on a hot tin roof."

"A little."

"Well, look, sugar, if it doesn't feel right, you don't have to—"

Jenna started laughing. "Merrilee, I'm twenty-nine years old. I obviously know how to say no."

Merrilee grinned. "Well, that's true enough now, isn't it. I guess my best advice is to just relax and enjoy yourself. If you're having a good time then he's having a good time."

Jenna checked her watch. Four more hours. The wait was almost over.

8

"THANKS FOR EVERYTHING," Logan said, nodding toward the basket. He'd picked everything out but Merrilee had put it all together for him. "It looks great." Logan put on his coat—he'd returned the loaner—and pulled on his gloves.

"I'm glad you like it. You made some good choices. Enjoy your evening." Merrilee hesitated and then added, "Jenna's a special person."

He'd reached that same conclusion. He'd read the "newspaper" article on her twice. "I think so, too, Merrilee. I think so, too."

It was the craziest thing. He'd *missed* her today. He'd caught a glimpse of her a couple of times this morning doing her thing in the front window at Curl's. As she'd pointed out, Good Riddance was so small, it was damn near impossible to avoid seeing her. However, catching a glimpse of her wasn't the same as actually spending time with her.

Carrying the basket in his right hand, he left through the front door of the B & B. Outside, snow danced down through the early evening sky. The temperature had dropped in the last hour since he'd returned to his room to shower and shave.

It was too early in the season for the aurora borealis display but he was certain it was an awesome sight to behold.

It had been a good day altogether. He'd enjoyed picking out the items for the basket. Leo, the dry goods store owner, was as sharp as a tack. He'd been as current on national and international business affairs as any other businessman Logan knew. Lunch with Norris had gone well—she had a slew of stories to tell after forty plus years in the newspaper business. And most importantly, Jenna's flowers had been delivered today.

Since Merrilee had told him, unequivocally there'd be no deal, he'd already sent the office an email and instructed Chaz to pursue the opportunities in Barton. As of this afternoon, he was officially on vacation.

As he walked along Main Street, he passed several people. Some he knew by name, others just from seeing them last night at Gus's. Everyone offered a friendly greeting. Logan wasn't sure he'd ever fully understand the town's rationale in passing up the kind of money his company had been offering, but he was beginning to get a small sense of their reasoning.

Jenna's front porch light was on and a feeling of homecoming ran through him. His place in Vinings had never actually felt like home. His mother had brought in a designer who'd shown him a couple of "storyboards" with colors and fabrics. He'd chosen one, then a couple of weeks and several thousand dollars later, he was set. But despite all the furnishings, there was an emptiness to his condo. He spent time there to eat, sleep and catch some mindless television, but there was never this sense of belonging that flowed through him now.

It must be Merrilee's talk about how special this place was. There was a lot to be said for the power of suggestion.

He knocked and stood there, waiting for Jenna to answer the door when he felt something brush against his leg. What the hell? He looked down. Tama rubbed Logan's leg again, offering a feline greeting. "Hey, big guy."

Maybe when he got back to Atlanta, he'd get a cat. That'd be cool. It'd be nice to have something to come home to. A cat could handle his occasional travel schedule and his long days at the office.

Jenna opened the door and all his breath seemed to lodge in his chest. She looked good, well, she actually looked great, but it was the expression in her eyes that nearly left him unable to breathe.

For what could've been a moment or a lifetime, his eyes locked with hers and he felt himself drowning in the oh-so-sweet emotion there.

"Hi," she finally said softly.

"Hi," he repeated, somewhat stupidly.

"Come on in."

He stepped into her cabin and she closed the door after him, enveloping him in the room's warmth and the scent of her perfume.

"You look beautiful," he said, feeling as gauche and awkward as he had at eighteen.

"Thanks." She smoothed her hand over her skirt and he got the impression she was as nervous and unsettled as he was. "You look nice, too."

"Thanks." He was glad he'd opted to wear khaki's and a buttoned-down shirt. Picnic or not, this wasn't a blue jeans and flannel kind of night.

"The flowers are beautiful," she said, sweeping her hand toward the vase that sat on the coffee table in front of the sectional sofa. The front door had opened into the den, but he'd been so busy looking at Jenna that he hadn't noticed anything except her at the time. "That wasn't necessary—"

"In my book, it was. The florist said yellow roses symbolize an apology. They're long overdue."

"You apologized last night."

"I wanted to send them, Jenna. I wanted you to have them."

"Then thank you." She seemed to notice the basket

he was holding for the first time. One of those radiant smiles that made him feel like he'd been kissed by sunshine bloomed on her face. "What have you got there, Logan Jeffries?"

He hefted the basket. "For our date tonight, how about an indoor picnic?"

"Ohhhh. What a ro...great idea." She'd almost said romantic.

He smiled like the idiot he seemed to morph into whenever he was in her company. He personally thought sitting on the hard floor was a bit loony, especially when there were perfectly comfortable sofas and chairs available, but if it elicited that kind of response from her, then he was all for floor-sitting. "Where should we picnic?"

"How about over by the pellet stove? It'll be nice and warm and there's lots of room."

"By the pellet stove it is," he said, grinning simply because he couldn't not, he was just so damn glad to see her.

"Right this way," she said, skirting the sofa. Lamplight glowed in the room and music he didn't recognize, but liked nonetheless, played low on an ipod docking station. "Nice music."

"Thanks," she said. "I wasn't sure what you listened to."

He placed the basket on the floor and did what he'd wanted to do all afternoon. Hell, what he'd wanted to do since he'd walked her home last night.

"Okay, let's start with hello again and do it right." He pulled her into his arms. She felt so right there, as if she'd been custom-made just for him. She tilted her head back, looking up at him, her lips parted in invitation. He kissed her. A short but thorough kiss that said how damn glad he was to see her.

"Hmm," he said. "That's better. But we might want to try it one more time to get it just right."

Her lips were even sweeter the second time around and he hadn't thought that was possible.

She was soft and warm in his arms and he held her close, reluctant to release her just yet. Her arms wrapped around his waist and she seemed content to stay in his arms. "This has been one of the longest days of my life," he said.

She tilted her head back, looking up at him, a teasing glimmer in her eyes. "It's the shorter hours of sunlight."

"That's not it!" He nuzzled her cheek and she burrowed against him.

"Then what made it such a long day?"

"You. This. You smell good. You feel great. And you taste even better." Another kiss, this one hungrier, more intense. She slid her hands up his chest, leaving a trail of fire in her wake, linking her hands behind his neck, her fingers stroking his nape.

She opened her mouth to him and he tangled his tongue with hers, giving himself over to the pleasure that was Jenna.

AN HOUR LATER, JENNA studied the angles of Logan's face in the candlelight. He'd confessed that the idea behind the picnic had been Merrilee's, but he'd done the shopping. She didn't care, it was still wildly romantic.

They'd spread the quilt on the floor and lit the candles he'd packed, setting them on the coffee table and end tables since that seemed to be the safest places in case Tama decided to investigate. So far, the cat had grandly ignored them and curled up in a laundry basket of towels off the kitchen.

At Logan's suggestion, they'd pulled the cushions off of the sofa so they had something to at least prop their backs against. It was relaxed, yet there was still a tension between them, the pull between a man and woman. She found him incredibly sexy, with his dark eyes and hair, a smile playing about his oh-so-sensual mouth.

They'd talked about how each of them wound up in their respective careers. Logan's had been predetermined at birth, while hers had been more or less something she'd pursued at the urging of her aunt Kate, who'd recognized Jenna's head for business.

"So, there's been nobody special in your life since you split with your fiancé?" he said. "I would have thought they'd be lining up from here to Anchorage."

Jenna smiled and sipped at her wine. "I wouldn't say all the way to Anchorage. Actually, I've just been, you know, happy to be hanging out here, enjoying being me. What about you? Any serious relationships? Or any that weren't so serious?"

"None of the above."

"Really?" She was incredibly relieved to hear it, although he could be lying. But he didn't strike her as the type. If he did, she wouldn't be sitting here with him now. "So, you're a nice looking guy with a good job, an okay personality—" she said that with a teasing note, causing him to nudge her with his toe and scowl "—all right, make it great personality, but you've managed to stay unattached. How'd that happen? Those Atlanta women must be slipping."

He sat there for a moment, studying his wineglass. He looked up. "Because none of them were you."

Her heart thumped against her rib cage. "You don't have to say that."

He looked faintly stunned. "I didn't realize it until…well, just now. I guess I hadn't really thought about it. I didn't have to make this trip. I'm not the one who handles acquisitions anymore. I came because I knew you were here. I'd seen it on Chelsea's Facebook page."

Was he saying he had followed her here? And if he'd found out about her through Facebook, then surely he'd known that she was relatively new to Good Riddance? "Logan, I lived in Marietta up until a year ago. I was right under your nose. Why did you wait twelve years to travel across the country to look me up?"

He looked at her sharply. "Did Merrilee tell you to ask me that?"

"No, I managed to come up with that all on my own. Why?"

"Because she asked me the same thing."

"Oh. And the answer is…?" Why now? Why wait all these years?

"I don't know."

"How can you not know?"

"I'm a guy, Jenna. I get up every morning and I go to work. I analyze numbers and come up with a bottom line. I don't sit around and think about relationships. I work with financials—numbers on paper. Plain and simple. Clear-cut. That's why I don't know."

"What about your family?"

"What about them? We're Jeffries. Not only do we not think about how we feel, we sure as hell never *discuss* how we feel."

"That's all my mother ever wanted to talk about. Her feelings."

"Maybe that's why she's been divorced so many times. Men aren't big into that."

Had he just said what she thought he'd said? "Hey, wait a minute. I can say that, but you're not allowed to."

"Why?" He really didn't get it.

"Because she's my mother, that's why."

"*This,* this is why men don't talk about feelings. Not only do we not know how we feel, but when we try and talk about it, we say the wrong thing. They should put warning labels on baby bottles for males—talk about how you feel with a woman and she's going to nail you."

Jenna sat for a second, processing his rant…and then she laughed. He looked at her as if she'd lost her mind. "You're right."

"Huh?"

"You're right. You're absolutely right."

"I am? You mean I didn't screw that up, too?"

"No." What difference did it make whether he knew how he felt? He was here with her now. And the last thing she wanted to do was argue with him.

"So, you don't want me to leave?" Relief showed on his face.

"Only if you'd rather be somewhere else. If that's the case, then yeah, I'd rather you leave. Just like if I wanted you to leave, I'd tell you."

"Okay. Good. Just for the record, I don't want to be anywhere else."

"That works, because I don't want you to leave. But I'd definitely like for you to kiss me again."

He put his wineglass on the end table behind him. She silently handed him hers. Logan leaned in close and buried his fingers in her hair. She sighed and rubbed her head against his strong hands.

He pulled her to him, nuzzling her cheek with his lips. "Jenna, you are the most amazing, fascinating woman."

She felt as if she was melting from the inside out. His words, his touch, his scent…

"Logan."

Her eyes drifted shut as he kissed her. He tasted like chocolate and wine. He sipped from her mouth, sampled her lips. She did the same, teasing and taunting him in return.

Desire moistened her thighs and left her breasts feeling heavy and needy. She wanted more than just his kisses.

He pulled her and she shifted until she was on his lap, her legs to one side on the floor. They shared hungry, eager kisses. He seemed intent to discover every nuance of her lips and mouth. His arms wrapped around her, warm and strong. She burrowed closer to the expanse of his chest, exploring the hair that curled over his collar, the edge of his jaw, the width of his shoulders with her fingertips.

He was like a potent drink, going straight to her head. He sprinkled kisses across her jaw, then nipped and sucked at the sensitive skin of her neck. Her breath came in short, hard pants and he stroked up the length of her leg with one of his hands, stopping just short of reaching beneath the hem of her skirt.

She wiggled until his hand slid beneath her hem and his fingers brushed against her thigh. A sweet liquid heat gathered in her sex. She'd wanted him so very, very long. She'd fantasized about him, about the two of them but his touch, his scent, his taste was so much more potent than anything she'd imagined.

She felt desperate to touch more of him, to be closer. She tugged at his shirt and loosened it from his pants. He was wearing a button-down with an undershirt on beneath it.

Jenna wasn't exactly sure how it happened but the next thing she knew, she was on her back and Logan was on top of her. And that suited her just fine. She liked his weight against her, his body heat, the press of his erection between her thighs. It was as if she couldn't get close enough to him.

Logan was like a fever she'd carried inside her for years.

"Logan, make love to me." He paused, his entire body going still except for the hard thump of his heart against her chest. The look in his eyes, a glittering heat combined with tenderness and wonderment, made her entire body tingle. "It feels as if I've wanted you for a lifetime."

"It's the same for me."

He sat up and took her by the hand, pulling her into an upright sitting position. "Where's your bedroom?"

She smiled, curling her fingers around his. "Across the hall." She stood, tugging him to his feet.

She felt too hot and tight for her skin, as if she would explode if he didn't release her.

Fingers intertwined, they crossed to her bedroom.

"Wait." She'd placed candles earlier today and she lit them now, her hand not quite steady. The room seemed to dance, a slow, erotic movement of candlelight on the walls and ceiling. She turned to him, silently holding out her hand in supplication.

He crossed the room, intent in his eyes. He took her hand and slowly brought it to his lips, kissing the back of it like a courtier in a movie. Deliberately, he turned her hand over and nuzzled the inside of her wrist. Sweet heat flowed through her.

It was as if they'd both waited so long, they wanted to take their time now and make it right. Without speaking he brushed his fingers along the line of her jaw. A tremor ran through her.

He feathered his fingers through her hair and molded them against her scalp. He gathered her to him and leaned his head against hers, his breath gusting warm against her skin. She closed her eyes at the unutterable sweetness of it, at the ache inside her he'd awakened. She inhaled his scent, a combination of man, soap and a hint of aftershave.

They stood together for what could have been seconds or hours, absorbing one another. He pulled off his shirt and then his undershirt.

She ran her hands over his chest, touching him, exploring him. She loved the contours, the feel of his skin covering hard muscles, the play of springy chest hair beneath her fingertips.

Jenna kissed the strong column of his neck down to his chest she'd just been exploring. There was no mistaking his shudder. "Oh, Jenna," he breathed against the top of her bent head.

Logan sat on the mattress's edge and eased back, pulling her down on top of him. She sprawled on him, reveling in the feel of him beneath her, the press of his jutting erection against her belly. She slid herself against his hardness and the sensation arrowed through her. She whimpered in the back of her throat.

Wrapping his arm around her, he rolled until they were on their sides and then he kissed her. She'd wondered if the earlier magic of his kisses would fade. So far it hadn't. If anything, this was even better than before. The comforter was cool beneath her, his skin was hot to her touch.

He kissed his way down her chest until he'd reached her breasts. "Jenna?"

She canted up and pulled the sweater over her head. "Yes. Please."

She smiled at the hiss of his indrawn breath. She wanted him as hungry for her as she was for him. He trailed one fingertip over her collarbone and down to the edge of her bra. This time *her* indrawn breath echoed in the quiet. She felt at once relaxed and yet coiled with tension at his touch.

He slid the straps down her shoulders, her skin on

fire where he touched her. His breath gusted warm against her as he leaned forward and kissed the tops of her breasts. Her heart hammered and her breath caught in her throat as he caught the cup of her bra in his teeth and tugged it down past her nipple. She held on to his shoulders as he swirled his tongue around the tip and she thought she might surely be dying a slow death at the feelings that swamped her. She ached. She rejoiced.

Jenna closed her eyes and arched up into his mouth, eager, needing what he was giving her. The moment he gently bit her tender point she nearly came unglued. It was the ultimate combination of slight pain and pleasure. He followed his love bite with a gentle lick and then suckled. "Oh…yes…"

It was as if she was caught up in a sensual dream. Logan stood. While he took off his slacks, underwear and socks, Jenna took off her skirt. Still wearing her panties, she laid back on the bed and looked at him.

He was everything she'd ever dreamed of and more. Lean but muscled, a smattering of hair on his chest arrowed down to a nice flat belly. But it was his penis that fascinated her.

Rigid with want, it jutted long and thick from a nest of dark hair, curved back toward his belly. In the flicker of the candles, a pearly drop of liquid dotted the tip. Trepidation warred with anticipation and excitement. She'd read books, seen pictures but was that going to fit inside her?

As if he sensed her shift in mood, Logan stretched out beside her. "Relax," he said and then kissed her, his tongue seeking the warm, wet recesses of her mouth even as he slipped his fingers beneath the elastic of her panties and stroked her.

"Oh, yes, yes, yes. Logan, I—"

She didn't even know what she was going to say, she simply knew she wanted more of that, more of him.

"I've got it taken care of, Jenna," he said as he pulled a condom out his wallet. Fever gripped her. She'd only thought she wanted him before. Nothing had ever prepared her for the maelstrom of emotion coursing through her, the tightness of her body, the tension that held her.

She wavered as he sheathed himself. Should she say anything or not? It was important to her, therefore, it should be important to him.

"Logan..."

He knelt, poised between her thighs. "Yes?"

She drew a deep breath and hoped he wouldn't think she was a freak. "I've never done this before."

His hands gripping her thighs tightened. "What? You mean you've never..."

"I've never done this before." She motioned to the two of them, naked, with him between her legs. "You're my first."

9

"ARE YOU SURE?" Logan said.

"I've never been surer." Jenna traced her finger along Logan's thigh, close to his erection. "And I didn't mean to stop things, I just wanted you to know. Tell me if I need to do anything I'm not doing."

"Honey, the only thing you need to do is relax. And tell me if you like or don't like what I'm doing."

"I've liked it all so far."

Jenna emphasized the fact by stroking along the length of his penis. He shuddered and clenched his jaw. "Jenna, honey, if you keep that up, we're going to be finished before we even get started."

She liked that he was as vulnerable to her as she was to him. "Then I guess I don't need to do that."

"Don't get me wrong. I love it when you do that. Do that another time. Right now I'm wound up too tight. And knowing what I now know about you, well that makes me even more tense."

"You don't think I'm a freak?"

He skimmed the back of his hand along her cheek. "You're a beautiful woman and I think I'm one lucky man. I'm honored."

Light and shadow played across the planes of his face. Jenna had never found a man more handsome and sexy than Logan Jeffries.

She rubbed her hands along his arms, his skin warm and supple. Her heart raced with excitement, her entire body quivered with anticipation. She had been waiting and waiting for this moment, not just the initiation into lovemaking, but *him,* Logan. Now that the time was here, she grew impatient. She lifted her hips in invitation and uttered one word, "Please."

Logan, too, was obviously tired of waiting. He nudged at her entrance.

Jenna closed her eyes as he slowly entered her. Leaning forward, he kissed her, absorbing her sharp intake of breath from the pain. A few moments later, however, her body stretched to accommodate him, in a good way. It was as if all of her nerve endings were centered on the sensation of him inside her, the press of his weight, his heat, his mouth on her neck, the brush of his hair against her jaw, the feel of his skin beneath her fingertips.

Logan began to move in and out, long, slow strokes. She'd never dreamed… "Oh, Logan, that feels so…good."

"Honey, you feel wonderful. Better even than I've ever imagined."

She hadn't thought it could get better but to hear him telling her he'd imagined doing this with her... "You've imagined this with me?"

His eyes glittered with heat and arousal as he made love to her. "So many times, so many different ways and the real you is so much better. Oh, sweet baby."

His words were like a magic aphrodisiac. She'd read that sex for women started in the brain. She'd just found the perfect combination—his words, which stimulated her brain, his body which stimulated her physically and his tenderness with stimulated her emotionally. And she knew exactly how he felt. "I've thought about you so many times, too. But...I...didn't...know it could be...so...good."

"Me, either. Me, either."

The strangest sensation gripped her. It was as if she were a spring, being wound tighter and tighter but at the same time she felt as if everything inside her, everything she'd ever known, was slowly unraveling, coming undone in the most delicious way.

Reaching between them, he stroked her. Pleasure so intense it bordered on pain filled her. Swallowing a gasp, Jenna closed her eyes but then opened them. She wanted to see him, watch him take this journey with her.

She didn't think she could take any more, but she

didn't want him to stop. She never wanted it to end, but she craved...something...she didn't know. She couldn't think, only feel.

"Jenna—" Logan's ragged voice held the same desperate note she felt. Slowly she spiraled higher and higher, losing control as she let herself ride the sensations, the feelings until she shattered into pieces. He quickly followed, her name echoing in the room as he found his own release.

Careful not to put all of his weigh on her, he nonetheless collapsed on her. And she knew she'd never be the same again.

LOGAN RETURNED FROM THE bathroom and slipped back into Jenna's bed, his heart still pounding. She smiled, a sensually lazy curl of her lips. He pulled her close to him and she snuggled against his side, her hair tickling against his still-damp skin.

He could hardly think straight. He looked up at the ceiling and tried to marshal his thoughts. Making love had never been like that ever before.

"Jenna." He didn't have anything in particular to say, he just wanted to say her name aloud. He smoothed his hand over her hair. She lay spooned next to him, her skin like soft velvet, her hair spilling against his shoulder. "Are you okay?"

"I'm better than okay."

"Can I ask you something? You were engaged?"

She seemed to know what he was asking. "Tad

had problems. So, he really was just as happy to not sleep together. He just wanted to have me on his arm."

"And before that?" He had to admit he was curious. She'd been responsive. Sex with her had been incredible so it wasn't as if she had a problem, or at least not one he'd seen.

She traced the birthmark, a kidney shaped darker patch of skin, on his chest with her forefinger. "My parents have both been married just a couple of times." She smiled at the irony of her parents numerous marriages. "From the time I graduated, I wanted to build a life for myself. I've seen so many women, my mother included, derail themselves by getting wrapped up in sex and relationships. And I guess I never found anyone special enough to put myself through that. It never felt right."

He smoothed his hand over the curve of her shoulder, her skin smooth satin beneath his palm. "And now?"

She swirled the tip of her finger against his wrist. "I never met another man who made me feel the way you do, who I wanted the way I wanted you tonight."

That was some heady stuff. And he'd never been anyone's first.

"Jenna..." Expressing himself, talking about how he felt didn't come easy to him. He didn't have any experience in that area, but dammit he'd try. "It's never been like this before, either. It's never been this good. You make me feel like no other woman's ever made me feel."

She smiled and pressed a kiss to his bicep. He wasn't through spilling his guts. "In school, I had such a thing for you."

"You did?"

"Uh-huh. Apparently I've still got a thing for you," he said, grinning. "Otherwise we wouldn't be naked in bed now."

"Excellent point."

When he left, he wanted to leave her with memories no other man could ever live up to. He wanted to be the first in every respect—the first to kiss every inch of her, to initiate her into the different rites of lovemaking. There was something about knowing no man had ever done the things he could do with her that made him want to bang his chest and swing from a vine.

He wanted to map her, explore her, chart her territory, find out what her most erogenous zones were so that he could know how to give her the most satisfaction.

"Jenna." He liked saying her name, the way it rolled off of his tongue. He trailed his fingers down her chest. "Your skin is so soft." Lightly, he traced the outline of her breast and then teased his fingertip around her pale-pink nipple.

She sighed, "Oh, Logan."

He smiled and leaned forward, licking the same

path he'd just touched. She shuddered and wrapped her fingers around his shoulder. Her soft noises of pleasure brought him satisfaction.

Shifting down the bed, he nibbled his way down her belly. He planted sucking kisses on the sweet spot of her hip. She wriggled beneath him and laughed. "That tickles."

He smelled her, the enticing scent of her arousal. Her pubic hair was trimmed close. He continued to kiss his way down her body, raising her leg to lick the skin just behind her knee. "Umm."

He spread her legs and lay down between them. Her woman's scent beckoned him. She looked at him, excitement glittering in her eyes.

"Put your legs over my shoulders, honey," he said, his voice harsh with the need to taste her.

Jenna did as he requested. It was like warm weighted satin draping over him. He closed his eyes, inhaling the fragrance uniquely hers. Opening his eyes, he sucked in an unsteady breath.

She was like a delicate flower opened before him, her petals glistening as if drenched by a summer rain. A need to bring her pleasure again, to satiate her, to render her mindless with ecstasy overwhelmed Logan. This wasn't about him. It was all about Jenna.

He teased his tongue along the delicate folds, gathering her sweet moisture.

"Oh," she gasped, her thighs tightening against his shoulders.

"Relax," he said in a soothing tone.

"I'll try, but that felt *so* good."

"It's about to feel a whole lot better," he said, not arrogant, just sure, her words stoking the fire inside him.

He bent his head and lapped at her, one long stroke against her silken channel. She uttered a gratifying moan. He tried different pressures, strokes, angles until he knew what she liked and how she liked it.

He tasted and teased and taunted until she was writhing, her hands clutching the sheets. "Please... now..."

He felt her tension mounting, her pleasure building toward a pinnacle. And it was heady stuff knowing he would be the one to take her there.

Within seconds she shattered, her hips moving as she spasmed beneath his mouth. Tasting her pleasure on his lips, her soft cries echoed in his ears like a sweet refrain.

JENNA LEANED DOWN to pull up the covers and was suddenly very much aware of muscles she hadn't even known were there. "Ow."

"Are you okay?" Logan looked at her with tenderness and concern.

"I'm fine. Just a little sore, but in a good way." She wondered if all lovers were as attentive and thoughtful as this man and then dismissed the idea. She'd heard too much girl talk to have such a foolish notion. She knew better. "That was definitely worth the wait."

He smiled, his expression faintly smug. Which was fine by her. He'd earned the right. She felt somewhere beyond good. "I'm glad you weren't disappointed. I have a feeling you'd have said so if you were."

"Oh, not disappointed at all. In fact, I'm looking forward to doing it again. Now I know what all the fuss is about."

"Good. So am I, um, you know, after some rest."

She laughed. "You're going to have to leave soon. I'm tired."

"Fair enough."

"But you don't have to get up and leave just yet." She liked this laying in bed together business. "You know the town's not going to sell out."

"Yeah. I do. Merrilee and I talked yesterday and then again today." He paused, a frown of speculation wrinkling his forehead. "Did you think sleeping with me…?"

"If I weren't so exhausted that might make me mad. But I'm too tired for me to get upset. Of course not. I slept with you because you turn me on. End of story."

He turned his head and smiled at her. "I'm glad I turn you on because you definitely do it for me."

Despite being tired, she felt a newfound playfulness with him. "How do you feel about that?" She laughed at the consternation that crossed his face. "Relax. That was a joke."

He laughed and rolled out of bed, getting to his feet. He snagged his briefs off the floor. "Okay. I don't know what your schedule is like but would you care to go cross-country skiing with me tomorrow?"

She settled on her side, watching him. He really was a beautiful man. "I'm afraid I'm going to have to pass." As he pulled on his underwear, she noticed the muscles in his butt flexing as he bent over. "I have the morning off but I've already got some things planned and I don't particularly like cross-country skiing. But we could get together again tomorrow night."

Logan tugged his undershirt over his head. "Sven invited me to play poker with him and some of the guys tomorrow night."

"No problem. I've got exercise class tomorrow night until eight. Gus's closes at ten. Just come over afterward."

He pulled on his jeans and looked at her as if he wasn't quite sure he'd heard her correctly. "You're saying that you don't mind if I play poker tomorrow night and then drop by after that?"

"Sure." She leaned over the edge of the bed and tossed his shirt to him.

He caught it one-handed and shrugged into it.

"You're good with us just getting together tomorrow night?"

It wasn't hard to figure out where he was coming from. "Logan, I want to get it on with you. We don't have to be connected at the hip. Well, I guess technically getting it on is being connected at the hip, but you get my drift. I've got a life. Just because we're good in bed together doesn't mean you've become the center of my universe. And I don't expect to be the center of yours, either."

He tucked in his shirt and zipped his jeans. "You're the most unusual woman I've ever met."

"If you say so." She'd seen other women throw everything away after hooking up with someone. Heck, her mother specialized in it. They met a guy and suddenly everything revolved around him. Only, it totally threw that person out of whack when there wasn't a him around anymore. Jenna had no interest in taking that path.

He sat on the edge of the bed. "Okay, here's a hypothetical question for you. Would you be upset if I forgot your birthday?"

This could be tricky. "Are we dating? I mean I know we're not dating now, we're just on a date. In your hypothetical situation, are we dating when you forget my birthday?"

"Yes."

"That's a no-brainer. Heck, yeah, I'd be upset if you forgot my birthday." She paused but he didn't ask when her birthday actually was. Okay, then. Clearly they weren't dating yet. "So, what does that prove?"

He reached over and pressed a quick kiss to her bare shoulder. "Nothing really. Only that we can lie in bed together and have an inane conversation."

Jenna liked this teasing side of him. She stifled a yawn. "Okay. It's just as well you're dressed because now I'm kicking you out." She climbed out of bed, picked her robe up from the chair in the corner of the room and pulled it on.

He wrapped his arm around her from behind, pulling her up against him. "I could come over for breakfast tomorrow morning, or is that putting me at the center of your universe?" His warm lips teased at a spot on her neck.

She leaned back into him. "Breakfast is fine. I've got to eat." She felt his smile against her skin. "How about you pick up a couple of Alaskan specials and I'll have the coffee ready?"

He turned her in his arms. "Oh, now I have to bring breakfast?"

"Well, of course." She blinked at him in mock innocence. "How else are we going to eat?"

"This cabin doesn't have a kitchen?"

"Of course it does. And you're welcome to use it. But since I don't keep much food in the house, you'd have to bring whatever you wanted to make."

He laughed. "Take-out's fine."

"Oh, good. Because now that I really think about

it, I don't have any pots and pans, either." They walked to the door and she saw him glance at their picnic still strewn on the floor. "Don't worry about it." It was amazing how good sex and two orgasms could tire a woman right out. "I'll return everything to Merrilee tomorrow."

"Okay. Two Alaskan specials. What time?"

"Let's aim for eight. I want to see what it's like in the morning."

"It?"

She stood on her tiptoe and whispered in his ear. "Us. Sex. Get plenty of rest tonight."

He hugged her tight and lifted her off the ground, kissing her good-night as he set her back on her feet.

"I've created a monster." His smile said he'd be ready.

10

LOGAN SIGNED OFF HIS computer the next morning. Even though he was officially on vacation, he'd checked and answered emails and taken a quick look at the financial markets. Some habits you just couldn't break. However, he was now officially on vacation.

Chaz had already lined up travel plans to Barton.

He headed down the hall to the communal shower. Luckily he was the B & B's only guest so there was no waiting for the bathroom.

Within minutes he was standing under the onslaught of warm water. Lathering up, he shook his head over Jenna's question about how he felt.

That just sounded like some getting to know his inner child nonsense. He knew what he thought and that was what was important. He thought she'd always fascinated him to a degree and that actually spending time with her would take care of that. He'd find she was just an ordinary person—a wonderful one, but ordinary—and he'd be able to put his fascination to rest.

Only that wasn't the case at all. Just when he thought he was getting to know her, figuring her out, nailing her down, he found out he'd only touched the tip of the iceberg. She, however, was no iceberg.

She had to be the most unique, intriguing woman he'd ever met. If anything, his fascination for her was increasing. The more he knew, the more he wanted to know.

He'd always lived his life according to plan. He'd never questioned the plan or the dictates—he just sort of rolled with the expectation. All his life he'd thought he was driven and on-course, but instead, he now knew he'd just been drifting along, never questioning or challenging, just doing.

On the other hand, Jenna didn't seem to live her life according to any rules except her own. She did what she wanted, when she wanted, how she wanted…because that was what she wanted. She was as much her own person as anyone he'd ever met and that was some damn potent stuff—being your own person.

It hit him. She thought outside the box, and lived outside the box while he'd spent his whole damn life crammed inside the box.

He turned off the water and grabbed a towel.

Maybe that's what came from thinking and never feeling. He'd be damned if he knew anymore.

If he was on vacation, maybe he'd just take a vacation from his life totally. Maybe for once, now that he'd figured out he'd been in the box, he'd step outside of it. What was the town motto? Something about leaving behind what ailed him. And while he was drawing on mottos and pithy sayings, how about "what happened in Good Riddance would stay in Good Riddance."

He realized one of the things he really liked about Jenna was that she pulled him out of his comfort zone. She always had. So, while he was here, maybe he should just embrace stepping out of his comfort zone for the next two days.

He reached for his shaving kit and then stopped. Nope. He'd give that a break as well.

A quarter of an hour later, dressed in jeans and a flannel shirt, he headed downstairs, his step lighter than it'd been in a long time, perhaps ever.

"Morning, Merrilee, Bull," he said, greeting the older couple.

Merrilee smiled, a knowing look in her eye. "Good morning. You're certainly looking chipper this morning."

"It's the first real day of my vacation." From his life, as he knew it. And it might've had something to do with having had stupendously great sex with an incredible woman last night. Not that he said that.

And not that he had to. He was pretty sure they'd figured it out.

"Good deal. Got any plans?"

"Breakfast at Jenna's—"

"From next door?" Bull said.

"Yep."

"She doesn't cook," Merrilee tossed in.

"That's what I hear."

"It's true." Merrilee poured a cup of coffee and handed it to Logan. "I walked her through baking boxed brownies once. Really, it's best if she just avoids the whole kitchen experience."

He grinned, inhaling the fresh-brewed aroma. "At least she knows her own limitations. Clint's taking me out cross-country skiing this afternoon and then I'm playing poker with Sven and the guys tonight."

"You need a cigar?" Bull said. "I have 'em flown in. A man is a better poker player when he has a good cigar."

"Thanks, but I'll pass," Logan said. "I appreciate the offer but Scotch is my poker weakness."

"You should stop by and see Bull's humidor over at the store. It's gorgeous," Merrilee added.

Bull nodded. "It was a gift from my wife, well, long before she was my wife." He put his arm around Merrilee, pulling her close. "It took me twenty-five years to convince her to marry me."

"That's a long time."

"I know. But I also knew from the first time I laid eyes on her she was the one."

"Kind of a feeling in your gut?" Logan spoke without thinking.

"Exactly. I think I'd have followed her to the ends of the earth if that's where she'd wanted to go. Finally, I had to put the ball in her court. I'd waited and waited but the next move had to be up to her."

Maybe it was a gust of cold air or something but gooseflesh prickled Logan's skin and his scalp tingled.

"Drop by this afternoon," Bull said.

"He wants to show off that spiffy humidor."

"Nothing wrong with that. Logan strikes me as a man of discerning taste if he came all this way to see Jenna, so I believe he'd appreciate it."

He gave up the fight. Fine, so he came all this damn way to see Jenna. He got it. Bingo. Bullseye. Denial dead and buried. "Thanks. I'll drop by later today."

He inched toward the door. "I guess I better go pick up breakfast. I don't want to keep Jenna waiting."

Merrilee burst out laughing and exchanged a look with Bull. "No, you definitely don't want to keep Jenna waiting too long."

Logan didn't get it. Obviously he'd missed something. Perplexed, he looked to Bull for an explanation.

"I know, son. Sometimes we're not meant to understand them."

But Bull had apparently gotten it. Whatever the joke, Logan let it go. He had a beautiful woman waiting on him.

JENNA HAD THE DOOR OPEN before Logan could knock. "Morning, stranger," she said.

"Morning, beautiful."

She closed the door behind him and wrapped her arms around his neck, kissing him good morning. She'd showered and dressed in a pair of white lace panties, her silk robe and nothing else.

"Mmm," he said. "You taste like mint."

She smiled, leading him toward the kitchen. "And you taste like coffee." She'd been turned on all morning. He'd been teasing with his monster comment last night but really, it wasn't too far off the mark. Now that she'd had him, she wanted more.

He put the take-out bag on the counter and turned to her, trapping her between him and the counter. She liked feeling the hard press of his body against the front of her and the solid counter behind.

There was something faintly predatory about his smile that set her pulse racing. "Now that I have both hands free, let's try this again."

This time their kiss was hot and hard and left no doubt as to what each of them had in mind. Logan caught her buttocks in his hands and squeezed. Jenna groaned into his mouth.

One kiss and her panties were damp.

"How do you feel about eating later?" she said, breathless, hungry for him.

"I think that's an excellent idea," he said. "Do you want to go to your bedroom?"

"No. Here. I've always had this little fantasy about doing it in the kitchen, maybe because I don't have any other use for the room."

"Oh, honey, I'm good with that."

She pushed his coat off his shoulders and he shrugged the rest of the way out of it, letting it drop to the floor behind him.

Dear God, he felt good and he smelled good and she wanted him with a desperation she'd never experienced. He kissed her again, his tongue exploring the recesses of her mouth. She arched against him, grinding her mound against his erection. Oh, yes.

He kissed her as if he wanted to devour her and she loved the intensity. It was as if he needed her as desperately as she needed him. She ached inside for him, for the closeness they'd had the previous night.

He dragged his mouth from hers and kissed along her jaw, down her neck. Her gasp echoed in the kitchen and she issued a breathy, "Yes." He bit lightly at the juncture of her neck and shoulder and the sensation arrowed straight through her, arousing her even more. He took her pebbled nipple in his mouth, robe and all, and sucked. She moaned her pleasure, her acceptance.

"You like that?" he asked, his breath hot against her skin.

"Yes."

He repeated it on the other side, leaving the material wet and cooling against her aching points.

She might've been a virgin up until last night, but she'd done plenty of reading and listening to other women. If you wanted something, you needed to let your man know. And she knew just what she wanted.

She reached between them and caught his hand in hers. Spreading her legs slightly, she guided his hand to the edge of her wet panties. "This is how much I like it." She slid his finger beneath the elastic and satin and he took over from there.

He tested his finger against her slick wetness and drew a shuddering breath. "Oh, Jenna. Baby, you're so wet," he whispered as he stroked her.

"I know. That's what you do to me."

He swooped down capturing her mouth with his, his kiss hot and hard as he fondled her. Sweet mercy, it was a different sensation from having him inside her but as good in a totally different way. His fingers were magic against her wetness. Then he inserted a finger inside her and she cried into his mouth, it felt so good. A second finger joined the first and she dug her fingers into the muscles of his shoulders.

With his fingers stroking in and out of her, he

found her clit with his thumb and Jenna truly thought she might die if he stopped what he was doing to her. "Please, don't stop…"

Now she was holding on to his shoulders because she wasn't sure if her legs would support her. He buried his fingers all the way inside her, his one finger rubbing a spot just inside her while his thumb continued to stroke and massage her. Tension mounted inside her until she thought she might explode…and then she did. She clung to him as he brought her past the brink of pleasure and she came in great waves.

When her orgasm finally subsided, they held on to one another, her breath coming in great gasps, his ragged against her neck.

"Oh, my," she said, feeling boneless and fluid and wonderful. "That was better than masturbating in a hot tub."

He looked at her, slightly dazed. "Huh?"

"I said that was better than masturbating in a hot tub. You know, when you've got that jet of water hitting you just right." She tilted her head back and looked up at him. "Well, I guess you wouldn't know. I'm sure it's different for guys but for a woman, you just sit in front of that jet and 'wow.' But it isn't as 'wow' as that just was."

"Well, I guess it's good that I feel better than pulsing water."

"It is. The water feels pretty darn good."

"Oh, yeah?"

"Heck, yeah. Why do you think so many woman dig a jetted tub? It massages a whole lot more than just a girl's back." There was a look on his face, an added glimmer in his eyes. "You know what I think?"

"What do you think?" His voice held a low, rasping note and he moved his finger against her thoroughly wet channel again.

"I think that idea turns you on, doesn't it?"

"You turn me on, but yeah, it does."

"I think you'd like to watch and then come in and finish up the job."

"Yes."

She reached between them and stroked her hand along the ridge pressing against his jeans. "Speaking of finishing up the job…" She unzipped his pants and reached inside his underwear, freeing his jutting penis. She ran her hand over the taut, velvet skin, feeling him tremble at her touch. A pearly drop of fluid gathered at the head.

She knelt before him. "Do you mind if I…"

Logan looked at her as if one, or both, of them had lost their mind. "Do I mind? Uh, no. Give me a second." He unbuckled his belt, unsnapped his jeans and tugged both his jeans and underwear down.

This time she backed him up against the counter. "Are you uncomfortable in here?"

"Honey, I'm fine if you're fine."

Jenna knelt in front of him, more than fine. This

was definitely a different perspective and she had to say, it looked a whole lot different up close and personal. It wasn't as if she'd never seen a penis before—well, as a matter of fact, she'd seen his last night but the bedroom had been fairly dark and it'd been halfway down her body.

Erotic and arousing, his sprang from a nest of dark, curly hair and curved. His balls hung full and heavy below. She leaned in closer, inhaling. She liked the way he smelled—a musky, masculine scent. Curious, she took him in her right hand and licked up the length of him. She liked the feel of him against her tongue and he obviously liked the feel of her tongue against him if his heavy sigh was anything to go by. She did that a few more times and then she took him in her mouth.

She'd been a little uncertain but she liked the taste and feel of him. And he'd made her feel so good, she wanted to do the same for him. She wanted to bring him pleasure. She wanted him to experience that same almost mindless satisfaction that he'd given her. And even though she'd just had an orgasm, she had to admit having him in her mouth turned her on all over again.

Her girlfriends had always been a divided camp—they either liked going down on their men or they didn't. There didn't seem any in-between. She was finding herself on the "like" side of the fence.

"Uh, watch your teeth, honey."

Oops. She worked her mouth and tongue over and around him, loving him, taking her cues from the sounds he made, which further excited her. There was something very erotic, very satisfying about bringing pleasure to your partner.

"Jenna, I…I can't. I'm going to…"

She stopped for a second. "Then do."

"You're sure?"

"There's only one way to know whether I like it or not and I like it so far." She took him back into her mouth.

Apparently that was the right thing to say because within seconds, she was tasting all of him against her tongue.

She liked it.

NELSON PUT ON A FRESH POT of coffee. Dr. Skye lived on the stuff and so did most of their patients but today was a slow day. He'd had to toss half the pot and start another one.

Clara Lightfoot, Ellie's grandmother, was scheduled for an arthritis check-up today. He was hoping Ellie would bring her in.

Ellie had been on his mind all morning. Most of the night, too, if he was being honest. The image of her in the water, the moonlight kissing her shoulders, her hair spread around her had invaded his sleep, haunted his dreams. He had seen Ellie in a whole different light.

The bell over the front door rang but it was Leo Perkins who entered. "Hi, Nelson. How goes it?"

"Pretty slow day. How about you?"

"Can't complain. Say, the missus sent over some molasses cookies. Been on a baking binge, she has." He held out an old-fashioned cookie tin.

Nelson took the box. Nancy Perkins made the absolute best cookies. "Tell Nancy thanks. You want a cup of coffee? I just made it fresh."

"Don't mind if I do." Leo helped himself to a cup and one of his wife's cookies.

Nelson snagged one as well.

Dr. Skye wandered out. "I thought I smelled cookies. And fresh coffee." While she poured herself a cup, she spoke to Leo. "How's the ingrown toenail?"

"Well, now that you mention it, it still hurts like the devil."

"I've got a few minutes. Come on back and let me have a look at it." Munching on a cookie, her mug in the other hand, Dr. Skye led Leo back to the exam room.

That was the kind of doctor he'd like to be.

Nelson was just emailing their weekly supply order when the bell over the door jangled. Ellie. He knew it before he saw her. Sometimes Ellie's mother was the one to bring in her grandmother, but somehow he'd known that today Ellie would be by.

"Hello, Nelson," Ellie's grandmother said, leaning heavily on the cane that helped her move with her arthritic knees.

"Good morning, Mrs. Lightfoot," Nelson said. He nodded to her granddaughter. "Ellie."

"Hi, Nelson," Ellie said. Her dark hair, in a loose plait, hung over one shoulder and past her breast.

"How about a molasses cookie and a cup of coffee?"

"Are they Nancy's cookies?"

Nelson nodded. "Leo just brought them in."

"I like Nancy Perkins' cookies. I'll take two," the older woman said, settling into a chair with Ellie's help.

"No, thank you," Ellie said. "But I'll make Aanak's coffee since I know how she likes it."

Something had changed since he'd shared the water of the lake in the moonlight and cold. Nelson felt a bond with Ellie, a meeting of spirit he'd never quite experienced with anyone before. It was as if they were communicating on another level outside of the mundane conversation in the office.

Two nights ago was special.

Yes, it was, wasn't it?

She poured the steaming liquid into a mug.

I want to swim with you in the moonlight again.

I'm looking forward to tonight.

She added creamer and some artificial sweetener and stirred.

I'll be there.

"Don't forget my cookies," her grandmother said, looking at the two of them, as if she was well aware of the nonverbal interplay going on.

Nelson grabbed a napkin and snagged a couple of molasses cookies out of the box. He delivered them, excusing himself. "I'll just step back now and see if Dr. Skye needs any help."

The truth of the matter was, if Dr. Skye needed help, she'd call for him. However, he wanted to escape Ellie's grandmother's discerning scrutiny before she saw too much. Especially since he didn't know exactly what it was he was afraid she'd see.

11

JENNA ROLLED UP HER YOGA MAT and waited while Merrilee did the same.

"Wow, I needed that," she said. The stretching had felt especially wonderful today and she always enjoyed the tranquil feeling afterward. It was like she revved up with zumba and then wound down afterward with yoga.

"So did I," Merrilee said, tucking her mat beneath her arm. Among a chorus of goodbyes, they stepped out into the dark for the walk home from the community center.

"I guess our men are deep into their poker game by now," Merrilee said. "So how did last night go? I wanted to get by all day but I was swamped. Logan certainly looked happy this morning."

Jenna smiled. "I had no idea what I was missing. The imagination doesn't begin to compare to the real thing."

"I'm glad to hear it. Not surprised, mind you, the way you two throw off chemistry, but glad."

"Merrilee, what do you make of someone who isn't comfortable with feelings?"

"Logan, I presume?"

"Yeah. He kind of had a freak-out when I asked him how he felt, so I dropped it."

"That discussion is pretty uncomfortable for most men. Give him time. It's like anything else. It's a new process that can be learned but can't be forced. Just let him be who and what he is. You can talk about your feelings all day, if that's what you need to do, just don't expect the same from him."

"You want to hear something crazy?"

"Sure."

The darkness made it easier to say. "I think I love him. And it's not just because of the sex, although that's pretty stupendous in my book, too."

"Tell me something I didn't know. The two of you are nuts about one another. So what's crazy about that?"

"Because I haven't seen him in twelve years. Because he's leaving in two days. Because there are a whole lot of things I don't know about him that might drive me crazy. I swore I wouldn't do this."

"Wouldn't do what, sweetie?"

"Fall in love with a man I didn't really know, only to find out later that he actually drives me insane."

Nothing had ever felt so right, but she'd also never been so scared of being wrong.

"You're not your mother."

"How do you know that's what she did? Do you want to know why she divorced my third stepfather? Because he left the toilet seat up. Don't you think she would've noticed beforehand?"

"Jenna, you are not your mother. You know who you are. Look at where you are now and I mean that in a literal sense. You just finished a yoga class."

"Uh-huh."

"If your mother had a new man in her life, would she be at a yoga class?"

Merrilee had a point. "No."

"Trust yourself, hon. Trust your instincts. Sometimes the heart recognizes what the head doesn't hear. Your heart told you from the beginning this was where you belonged. Perhaps you waited for twelve years because, once again, your heart knew. Wherever the path leads, be true to yourself."

"Okay, but what about Nelson? Remember how I sort of had that crush on him? How trustworthy is my heart if I felt that way then?"

"Your heart recognized him as a friend, a kindred spirit. It was simply your head that had it confused. I don't believe for a minute your heart is sending you the same message about Logan that it sent you about Nelson."

"Um, well, no."

"Sometimes we have to get out of our own way, Jenna." She paused for a second, her smile rueful. "Look at me and Bull. Talk about having to get out of my own way..."

The truth of the matter was that Logan meant so much to her, she was scared to even consider the possibilities. She so badly wanted what she thought they could have. And she was afraid they wouldn't get it.

ELLIE SHIVERED. SHE WAS COLD.

In all the years she'd been coming to Mirror Lake, she had never been chilled when she was drying off. Perhaps it was because she'd stayed in the water far longer than she normally did, waiting on Nelson. She had thought if she just stayed long enough, he would show up. But hours later, she was still alone in the water.

She'd always found great comfort in the lake but not tonight. Instead of being soothed by the slide of thermal water against her skin and the gently falling snow, she'd been preoccupied, waiting on a man who had never arrived.

She cranked her jeep and rubbed her gloved hands together. Chugach sat in the passenger seat. "I am a foolish woman," she said to the dog. He regarded her with knowing, watchful eyes.

In her mind, she and Nelson had shared a connection today. She could've sworn they'd been on the same plane. She played it back through her head again as she shifted gears and turned around. He'd said last night that he'd come back. And although the words hadn't left his mouth, he'd said it again today in the clinic as clearly as if he'd spoken aloud.

Yes, she'd been foolish on many levels. One, to think that he'd actually show up. Two, that she'd stayed in the lake that long. And thirdly, she had allowed her thoughts of him to superimpose themselves on the experience itself, so that the peace and answers she usually found in the water had been nonexistent.

She heard a hum and lights in the distance. Someone was coming. Her heart began to pound in her chest. She pulled to one side, being careful not to go so far that she'd land herself in the ditch. The other vehicle rounded the curve and it wasn't until it drew nearly even that she could see past the headlights. It was Nelson. He had come!

He pulled even with her and they both lowered their windows. Shadows obscured his face.

"I didn't think you'd still be here," he said.

What? Had he waited, giving her plenty of time to clear out? God, she'd been totally stupid. Hurt and anger swamped her. "I was just leaving." Even though she tried to keep her response normal, her voice sounded stiff. She didn't really care, as long as she didn't cry in front of him. Only she was dangerously close to doing just that.

"No. I didn't mean it that way, Ellie. I got called out to check on Darren Whitefeather. I didn't *think* you'd be here, but I *hoped* you would."

"We almost weren't. Chugach and I were heading home." He looked almost crestfallen. "But I've got a few minutes if you needed to talk."

"I'd like that," he said.

She suddenly felt ridiculously, immeasurably better. "I'll go to the main road and turn around. I'll meet you at the top of the hill."

She caught a flash of his teeth as he smiled. "I'll be waiting."

Although it was but a short distance, it felt as if it took forever for her to drive to the main road, turn around and stop next to him on the hill that served as Mirror Lake's parking spot. Her hands and legs were unsteady as she killed her engine and climbed out. "Stay, Chugach."

The dog settled on the seat, content.

She opened the passenger door of Nelson's truck, the dome light coming on, and got in. It was much warmer in his vehicle than hers, but that's because her engine hadn't had time to heat up yet.

"You look tired," she said.

The light went out and once again the shadows claimed him. "It's been a long day. And then I was ready to come out here when I got the call about Darren." Taking "sick" calls was part of his training to take over as the clan shaman. "I would've let you know but I don't have your number."

"I can remedy that if you have a piece of paper and pen," she said. "Although sometimes I don't get service out here."

He turned on the dome light again and handed her a notepad and pencil. "But at least I could've left a message so you didn't think I was a no-show." She felt him watching her as she wrote down her number. "That is what you thought, wasn't it?"

Her grandmother had always told her she wore her feelings on her face. Apparently she still did. "The thought crossed my mind."

"I wouldn't do that, Ellie."

She handed him her number. "That's good to know."

He turned off the light, leaving them in the dark once again. Outside, snow fell, melting as it encountered the warm windshield. Inside, an easy silence stretched between them.

Ellie sat, content to share the cab with him, to inhale the scent of wood smoke and antiseptic that clung to him. It took her a second to realize that his breathing had become steady and deep. She leaned forward, bridging the space between them and peered at him.

Nelson had fallen asleep. She smiled quietly to herself. At least he was comfortable with her, although that wasn't what she particularly wanted. Just once she'd like to incite a man to great passion. Too bad it wasn't going to be this man on this night.

LOGAN FELT GOOD—ALL WAS pretty damn right with his world. He'd just lost fifty bucks to Sven, but he'd had a good time doing it, drinking damn fine Scotch and smoking an even finer cigar. And now he was on his way to see Jenna.

Once again, as with the night before, her porch light glowed with welcome, a homecoming. He knocked and she opened the door, greeting him with that sunny smile that undid him every time. "Hi." She stepped aside for him to enter, then closed the door behind him. "How was the poker game?"

"Good. How was yoga?"

"It was fun."

"Uh-huh."

He backed her against the door and kissed her thoroughly.

"Um. You taste like whiskey…and you. I like it."

"I'm glad."

She ran her hand over his jaw. "Good Riddance is turning you into a real reprobate. Did you skip your daily appointment with the razor this morning.

"How do you know I shave every day at home?"

"Do you?"

"Yes." Smarty-pants.

She smiled. "I thought so. Logan, do you leave the toilet seat up?"

Really, he was learning that with Jenna it was best not to worry about following her train of thought. He probably wouldn't follow the rationale anyway. "I'm a guy and I live alone, so yes. But when I'm in someone else's house, no."

"Okay. And do you put the toilet paper on so that it rolls down from the front or from the back?"

He had to think about it for a second. "Back."

"Don't you want to know which way I do it?"

"No. My needs are simple. I don't care which way it rolls, as long as it's there when I need it. How am I doing so far?"

"Well, enough."

"That doesn't give a guy a whole lot to go on."

"You're here, aren't you?"

"True."

He knew it was a dead end but he asked anyway. "Do you ever think about moving back to Georgia?"

"I'm building a business here."

"So? You have a business there, as well."

"But here, it's more than a business. It's my home. Let me show you something."

She took him by the hand and led him to the sofa. "Sit." He sat.

Grabbing a roll of blueprints from the corner, she flipped on the overhead light. She unrolled the papers on the ottoman. "Here's the spa. Reception area, nail salon, hair area, massage room, sauna, whirlpool, storage and laundry facilities. Up here is the living space. Very small kitchen, den, guest room, bath and then up here, a loft bedroom with a walk-in closet," she said, pointing.

"What about a family?" Surely someone with Jenna's warm, giving disposition wanted a husband and kids. The thought made him ache inside. If he fell into the next phase of the Jeffries plan, he'd be looking to start his own family soon enough back in Atlanta.

"I can always build up."

"True." It was far too easy to imagine her laughing and playing with a couple of kids. She'd be a fun mom.

She rolled the blueprints back up. "Moving back isn't on my radar."

"I can see that. You just don't seem like the wilderness kind of woman." There was a part of him that just couldn't concede it. "You don't even like cross-country skiing, for crying out loud."

"So? Do you like to bowl?"

"No, I can't say that I do."

"Okay, then. There are a lot of bowling alleys in your area. When's the last time you went to an art museum or a play?"

"Okay, okay. I get you."

"Have *you* ever considered moving?"

He didn't hesitate. It had never even crossed his mind. His life was centered in Atlanta. "No. My family's there, my job is there, my life is there."

Jenna nodded. "I know."

"So what was with the twenty questions earlier?"

"Hardly twenty. Try two. Can't a woman be curious? I'm just trying to get to know you. The real you. The important you."

"Yes. I've always thought I was defined by how I loaded my toilet paper dispenser."

"So, what do you think defines someone?"

"How do you manage to ask these difficult questions?"

She laughed, her eyes alight with humor. "Think about it and get back to me later." Her expression sobered. "Logan, I—" She hesitated and cupped his face in her hands. "I'm glad you're here. I'm glad you came. I'd like it if you stayed tonight."

What she didn't say, he saw in her eyes, in her expression, in her tenderness. She loved him. And the hell of it was, he didn't know how he felt about that. He didn't know how he felt about her. So he said the only thing he could. "I'm glad I'm here, too. And I'd like to stay…tonight. You matter to me."

It was the best he could do. He had no idea if it was enough.

JENNA WOKE TO FEEL THE PRESS of Logan's body next to hers. For a minute she simply lay there, absorbing, reveling the experience. She'd never spent the night with a man in her bed like this.

Of course, she and Tad had shared a bed when

they'd come to Good Riddance but that had been different. She felt kind of strange lying in bed with one man and thinking about another but it wasn't as if she was thinking of Tad with longing. She was simply reflecting on what their situation had been.

But this, having Logan next to her, was how it should be—his steady, even breathing against her shoulder, the warm strength of his arm wrapped around her, the solid press of his body against her back. She could wake up like this every morning for the rest of her life. True, she didn't know what his favorite color was or who his favorite sports team happened to be, but none of that mattered.

She'd categorized it as a teenage crush but she'd fallen in love with him years ago. Somewhere inside, she'd avoided other men because she'd been waiting for Logan. But where was a future there?

She peered at the clock. Six-thirty in the morning. She was glad he'd stayed the night. She was glad he was in bed with her now.

She shifted, not wanting to wake him. But she needed to see him sleeping in her bed. To remember what it was like. Her heart seemed to turn over. He was so sexy. The dark stubble covering his jaw and cheek combined with his tousled hair was a good look on him. The covers had slipped down leaving his broad shoulders and part of his nicely muscled chest bare.

Desire bloomed low in her belly. Simply looking

at him tripped her trigger. She leaned forward and kissed the side of his neck. She'd discovered last night it was a hot spot for him.

"Um," he murmured, "good morning."

"Morning," she said, teasing her tongue against his shoulder.

He blinked his eyes open. "Are you—"

"I am." She rubbed against him. "I thought we could hop in the shower. I could wash your back and any other hard-to-reach parts and you could do the same for me."

He skimmed his hand over her bare hip to cup her buttock in his hand. "I like the way you think."

A sudden, loud knocking on the door interrupted them. No one ever knocked on her door this time of the morning. She threw back the covers as another harsh rap sounded. "Coming," she yelled. "Hold on a minute."

Logan switched on the bedside lamp, a questioning look on his face.

"I don't know," Jenna said, grabbing her robe from a chair in the corner. Foreboding filled her as she shrugged into it and knotted it at her waist, already halfway across the room.

Logan was up and pulling on his jeans.

She hurried to the door and threw it open. Merrilee and Bull stood outside wearing grim expressions, tears shimmering in Merrilee's eyes. Please

God, don't let anything have happened to her family was the first thought that raced through Jenna's mind.

They came in, Bull closing the door behind them. Merrilee, regret and sympathy on her face, took Jenna's hand in hers. She sensed Logan coming to stand at her shoulder.

"Is my family okay?"

"Yes, honey, your family's fine. Everything's going to be okay but, I don't know how to tell you, there was a fire…" She motioned in the direction of the spa.

Jenna realized, as if all of her senses hadn't been totally present, that the acrid smell of smoke had entered with Bull and Merrilee.

She knew, inside, before Merrilee even spoke the words.

"The spa is gone."

LOGAN WAITED, STANDING TO THE side, feeling helpless, his heart breaking for Jenna as she stood surveying the smoldering shell that was her dream. Falling snow sizzled against the blackened timbers.

Most of town stood to one side, watching silently, a force of support.

"Does anybody know what happened?" she finally asked, breaking the silence.

Merrilee shook her head, "I've already called. A fire investigator from Anchorage is flying in today to figure it out."

Jenna nodded and turned her back to the ruined structure. She looked faintly surprised to see all the people who'd gathered in the dark morning. Her eyes found Logan's, connecting for a moment and then she looked back to the townspeople. "Thanks, everyone. I guess there's not much we can do for now. I appreciate you all being here."

"You need anything?" Leo asked, Nancy by his side.

"Thanks, Leo, but I'm good."

The group began to disperse. Logan put his arm around her, inviting her to lean on him, draw strength from him. It wasn't much, but it seemed the least and the most he could do under the circumstances. He glanced at her, trying to read what she wanted, what she needed. She sent him a thankful smile, reaching down to grasp his gloved hand in hers.

Sven ran his hand over his head. "You need some time or do you want to talk about this now?"

"Now is as good a time as any," she said.

"Do you need me?" Merrilee said, her look encompassing both of them. Logan liked being included.

"No," Jenna said, "you've got plenty to do between the B & B and the airstrip." She squeezed his hand. "We'll stop by later this morning."

"Okay."

Teddy came up, offering a quick, hard hug. "I'll

run breakfast and a thermos of coffee over. How many breakfasts do you need?"

"Just three." Jenna looked at Logan. "Can you stay while I talk to Sven?"

If she wanted him there, he'd damn sure make time. "Sure."

Teddy looked from Jenna to him. "Okay. Three breakfasts coming your way. Everybody good with the Alaskan?"

"That works for me."

"Me, too."

Sven simply nodded, his usual smile absent. Of course, he was looking at a couple of months of work lying in a rubble heap. Jenna looked at it as well, shock seeming to set in.

"Thanks, Teddy," Logan said, taking over. Jenna needed coffee, food and a chair and not necessarily in that order.

The bitter smoke hung in the air as they walked down the sidewalk, past the dry goods store, the video/screening room, the bank, the taxidermy business that doubled as a mortuary, barber shop and Jenna's current nail business.

"Looks like I'll be there a while longer," she said as they passed it.

They made the rest of the trip in silence. It wasn't until they got to her cabin and were sitting at the kitchen table that Jenna squared her shoulders and looked at Sven. "When do you think you could start back on it?"

He cocked his head to one side. "Really, realistically, you're looking at late spring. I know it's not what you want to hear, but…"

Her enthusiasm aside for moving into her own home, Logan sympathized most with her lost revenue stream. Particularly as she would miss out on the lucrative Chrismoose festival and Christmas season.

Jenna picked up the conversation as she opened a can of cat food for Tama. "Because of the cold?"

"We mainly work interior jobs in the late fall and winter. That was why we had your interior scheduled for now. To start building from the outside all over again…" He shook his head. "Getting the materials here would be tough enough, logistically, and it's really too cold to build this time of year. Not only are there equipment issues, but injuries are more likely to occur."

Jenna tapped her finger against her chin, obviously running through some mental calculations. "I've got bookings that start in mid-December, so that means at least four months of lost income."

"Will your insurance cover part of that? I'm sure this has happened somewhere down the line before," Logan added.

Jenna shot him a grateful look. "I'll check when I call this morning. Good idea." She shook her head. "I'm not thinking so clearly right now."

That was more than understandable.

There was a knock on the back door and Logan jumped up. "I'll get it. You two keep talking."

Teddy stood outside with a box. Logan stepped aside and she entered the kitchen, placing the parcel on the counter. Logan helped her unload the three to-go boxes and one of the biggest thermoses he'd ever seen.

"Thanks," Logan said as Teddy started back to the door.

"Yeah, thanks," Jenna offered from the kitchen table. "I'll stop by and take care of the bill later."

Teddy waved a dismissing hand. "It's on the house, Lucky said. That's the way we roll at Gus's."

"Then tell him I said thanks."

Apparently that was the way they rolled in Good Riddance, Logan realized. People hadn't been gathered around this morning to gawk, they'd been there to help in whatever way they could.

Logan closed the door behind Teddy and rounded up coffee cups. He brought everything to the table. Jenna shot him a grateful look.

Sven stood. "If you don't mind, I'm going to take mine back to my place and start looking at some numbers."

"No problem. We'll talk later."

When the door closed behind Sven, Logan automatically reached for Jenna and drew her to him, wrapping his arms around her. He'd been wanting to hold her from the moment Merrilee had broken the news. She rested her head against his chest, leaning into him.

"You were pretty amazing this morning." She'd displayed both strength and grace under extenuating circumstances.

"Thank you, Logan, for staying. For being here."

"Whatever you need, Jenna. Whatever you need." They stayed that way for several moments, him holding her, her leaning into him. He smoothed his hand over her head. "I know how important the new business was to you," he said against her hair.

She nodded. "It was. It is. I'll regroup and it'll all work out. The main thing is that no one was hurt. That would've been hard to deal with."

"I'm impressed with how calm you are."

"Really?" She offered a smile, one that made him feel as if he was turning inside out. "I guess I just learned early on that life happens and you just have to roll with it."

"That's a good philosophy."

"It's worked okay for me. By the way, your eggs are getting cold."

He didn't give a damn about his eggs or anything else but her right now, but maybe she was hungry. "Which means your eggs are getting cold, too."

She traced the line of his jaw with her fingertip, a soft look entering her eyes. "I'm not particularly interested in eggs, cold or otherwise, right now." Her expression said she wanted him to make her forget her dreams had just gone up in smoke. Her eyes asked him to distract her until she was ready to deal with the loss.

For one horrible, traitorous moment, he thought that now with the spa gone, she wasn't tied here. But that wasn't true. Building or not, this was clearly where she belonged.

"Let's go back to bed," he said, leading her toward the bedroom.

He'd give her whatever she needed. Until he had to leave.

12

JENNA LAY IN THE DARK, in her bed, curled next to Logan. She could tell by his breathing he was awake as well. Neither one of them had slept all night. It was as if neither of them wanted to squander their last few precious hours on sleep.

They'd talked about life, their families, their futures. Logan had told her very honestly he would be expected to marry and produce an heir. It was the Jeffries way. The very thought made her heart ache to an almost unbearable degree—the thought of someone else sharing his life, his dreams, his bed, his future. But at least he'd been honest. They'd alternately talked and made love throughout the night. They'd been rough and needy one time, tender and romantic the next. They'd tried to cram the rest of a lifetime into those last few hours.

"Logan?"

"Yes?"

"Did you sleep any?"

"No. You?"

"None."

Following her own path, Jenna spoke the words that wouldn't be contained any longer. "I love you, Logan. I've loved you for a long time."

Her words settled between them, like golden leaves that drifted down to cover the sidewalk on an autumn day.

"Jenna." His voice was even and quiet. "You know I have to leave."

She hadn't told him to elicit a response. She'd simply told him because love was a gift to be given. "This isn't about you staying or leaving. It just is what it is."

"You know I care about you."

"I know that." And she did. She felt it in his touch, in the way he looked at her, in the strength of his arms around her yesterday after the fire. "I've known since the day you sent those roses."

"You have?"

She loved him, but he could be truly clueless. "You know, Logan, for such a smart man…"

He laughed softly in the dark. "I know."

"You know what Merrilee told me yesterday?" She splayed her fingers against his chest, touching him while she could. "She knew exactly what your scout wanted when he came to check out the town. She knew his purpose from the moment he stepped in the door. But you threw her. She didn't associate you with the gold. You know why? Because she sensed why you were really here. She knew you were here for me. So did everyone else in town."

He sighed. "Maybe every couple of months we could—"

"No, Logan, that's no way to live, like we're one another's quarterly obligation that gets penciled in on the schedule. We both deserve more than that."

"I thought you said you loved me."

"I do. I always will." What she felt for him ran soul-deep. "But that's not fair to whomever you start to date when you get back. And I'm certainly not going to be the woman on the side. I either want all of you or none at all."

"Fair enough. Have you ever thought that the spa burned down for a reason? That you're free to go?"

Of course the thought had crossed her mind, but she'd concluded otherwise. "I'm free to go regardless, Logan. I choose to be here because this is where my heart belongs. You are who my heart belongs to, but this is the physical mailing address attached to that organ."

"You'll let me know on that other issue?" The condom had broken last night and she was having a hard time knowing if that was good or bad. Time would tell.

"Of course I'll let you know. And we need to be clear that I'd never deny you access to your child, but I will also never turn my child over to become a little Jeffries automaton."

"Just let me know." She'd hurt him with that last bit. She hadn't meant to but dammit, she was hurting, too.

She only knew one thing that could heal them both. Granted it wouldn't change the outcome, but it would heal the hurt.

"Logan, one last time—"

He was already reaching for her before she got the last word out of her mouth. "Make love to me like you're never going to make love to me again."

And there in the dark, silently, he did. With touches and kisses, they expressed something that ran far deeper than words. Jenna gave him a part of her to carry with him, a part of her that would always be with him. And Logan, her sweet, sweet Logan, so fearful of his own feelings, gave her the same, a measure of love that refused to be compromised by time, distance or circumstances.

LOGAN CLIMBED ONBOARD THE puddle jumper and didn't look back. Dalton climbed into the pilot's seat and readied them for take-off.

The normally exuberant sky jockey was quiet, which suited Logan just fine. He patted his laptop for probably the fifth time since checking out of his room. He had the unshakeable sense of leaving something important behind.

Jenna hadn't come to the airstrip to see him off. They'd exchanged their goodbyes privately this morning. He'd be damn glad to shake the dust of Good Riddance from his feet. Sure he'd seen the charm of the town. He'd felt the same draw, the sense of camaraderie that was so seductive to the citizens that they'd opt to struggle financially just to stay there. He'd had a taste of it. Still, this morning, everyone he'd met had looked at him with a measure of pity in their eyes. Anger? Censure? Disappointment? He could handle all of that, but *pity?*

That was fine. Perhaps they'd all been in situations that allowed them to just up and move to the middle of the Alaskan wilds. Not a damn one of them walked in his shoes. None of them understood his life was solidly grounded in Atlanta, full of obligation and expectation.

The day, as was befitting his mood, was gray. The clouds hung low and dark. The little plane, cleared for take-off, rolled down the runway and lifted into the overcast morning.

Good riddance to Good Riddance.

Logan pulled out the spread sheets for Barton and reviewed them during the trip to Anchorage. He already knew the information—it was his job to know the numbers—but he refreshed himself once again.

Soon enough Dalton landed the little plane at Anchorage. He climbed out onto the tarmac and handed Logan's luggage off to him.

"Take care of her," Logan said, speaking from his heart.

Dalton looked momentarily surprised and then he broke out his familiar grin. "Jenna's going to be fine. You're the one we're all worried about."

What was there to say to that? Nothing.

Logan turned and walked away.

NELSON FINISHED UP at the office, impatience coursing through him like the frozen river beginning to thaw in spring.

He poked his head in the doorway of Dr. Skye's office. She sat behind the desk, busily making notes. Looking up, she smiled wearily, her curly red hair its usual mess. It hadn't always been thus.

Nelson thought how nothing stayed the same. When Skye had come to Good Riddance a year ago as a temporary fill-in for the town's regular doctor, she'd been a different woman, her hair rigid and straightened into submission because that's the way she'd been told it should be.

"You've been somewhere else all day," she said, setting aside her pen.

"I'm sorry. I didn't think—"

"Nelson, it wasn't a complaint. I was merely making an observation. Do you want to talk about it?"

He shook his head. "It is nice of you to offer but the answers I seek aren't to be found within these walls."

She had come to know him as a good and trusted friend. Her respect for the boundaries of that friendship were evident as she acknowledged his unspoken quandary. "Then I hope you find the answers you seek wherever they may be."

"Thank you. I'll see you tomorrow."

She picked up her pen, already switching gears back to the patient charts before her. "Have a good evening, Nelson."

"You, too."

Nelson was shrugging into his jacket when the office door opened and Dalton strolled in. "Is my wife almost ready to call it a day?"

"Close but no cigar."

Dalton grinned. "Are we going to see you at dinner tonight?"

"Not tonight."

"Hot date?"

Nelson thought of the thermal lake and smiled. "More like warm date."

"Enjoy Mirror Lake." Nelson's surprise must've shown on his face. "After all these years, I get the subtle inside humor."

"Yes, you do. Keep it under wraps if you would— my location that is, not the getting it," Nelson added.

"You've got it."

Nelson left the clinic, got in his truck and headed out of town, eager to reach the lake and Ellie.

Nelson had actually thought about discussing his

dilemma with Dalton but Dalton wouldn't fully understand because of the culture difference. However, Dalton would know what it was like to make a choice that everyone in your family disapproved of. In their own way, Dalton's family had done the same thing to him, ostracizing him when he'd given up his corporate job and his fiancée to move to Alaska and be a bush pilot. Nelson supposed that in every culture a man could find a clash between tradition and free will.

He turned off of the highway and bumped along the rough track leading to the lake. It didn't look as if anyone had been here before him. He turned the corner in the road and sure enough, Ellie's jeep wasn't anywhere to be seen. He'd obviously beaten her here.

He got out of his truck and released his hair from the leather thong tying it back. The wind blew through it, shifting it about his shoulders and across his face, a caress of the elements.

He was not a man to either quick or impulsive actions. He never had been. He had been born under the mark of the bear. It was his nature to contemplate, hibernate inside himself until he found the answers he sought to move forward. For all his uncertainty and indecision, he did know one thing with absolute surety. When Ellie Lightfoot arrived, he intended to kiss her.

JENNA WALKED DOWN THE sidewalk, soaking up the last of the sun's rays. The days were getting shorter and shorter, the nights longer and longer.

Donna was in the dry goods store. Jenna waved at both her and Nancy. Merrilee fell into step beside her. "How're you doing?"

"I miss him."

"I know, honey, I know."

"I understand that he's got to follow his own path, but I sure wish he'd wake up sooner rather than later." Even keeping busy with the insurance company, dealing with the fire damage and contacting everyone from clients to vendors about the delayed opening didn't keep Jenna from missing him. And she was simply exhausted these days.

Merrilee rubbed her arm. "Bull didn't give up on me. You can't give up on him, Jenna. Anyway, what else are you going to do? Just the same thing you're doing now. So you might as well not give up."

"Hope springs eternal in the hearts of lovers and fools."

Merrilee laughed. "Darlin', I believe that'd be hope springs eternal in the human breast."

"I like my version better."

"Okeydokey. Where are you off to?"

"I've got an appointment with Skye. I've been a little under the weather."

"Things are dead over at the airstrip. I'll go with you if you want me to."

Jenna was pretty sure she knew why she was feeling under the weather and having Merrilee along was just fine with her. Logan should be the one here but that obviously wouldn't be the case.

Ten minutes later Jenna was sitting back in the exam room on the patient table while Merrilee had taken the straight chair in the corner.

Skye came in, Jenna's chart in hand. Other than a wicked cold last year, Jenna had never been in to see Skye professionally. "So, you're feeling a little under the weather?"

"Can you run a pregnancy test?" Jenna said, cutting to the chase.

It was a testimony to Skye's professionalism that she merely blinked her surprise before she recovered and slipped back into doctor mode. "Certainly."

Merrilee, however, after a moment of stunned silence said, "Merciful heavens. Didn't you use…?"

"One broke."

"Well, let's find out. How late are you?"

"I don't really know. I don't keep track because I hadn't been sexually active until lately."

"Okay, well, we'll start with a urine test. If you can step into the bathroom and give us a sample, we'll give you an answer."

Jenna stepped into the bathroom and made the requested urine donation.

"Honey, I can't believe you didn't mention this," Merrilee said when Jenna came back into the room.

Sitting up on the exam table, Jenna shrugged. "There really hasn't been anything to mention—"

Skye came in. She looked at Jenna, a smile in her eyes. "Well, you'd better start thinking about names. It's positive. You're going to be a mother."

Even though she'd suspected, in fact she'd been pretty sure, Jenna still felt stunned. "I'm pregnant?"

"You're pregnant," Skye said.

"You're pregnant," Merrilee echoed as if she couldn't quite believe it.

She was going to have a baby.

And not just any baby. Logan's baby.

LOGAN SAT AT HIS DESK AND thought about calling. Or emailing. Or Skyping. He'd been back four weeks. Make that four, long miserable weeks.

Nothing had changed at the office. His condo remained the same. His family was just as uptight and remote as ever. So, if nothing in his life had changed, then why the hell was everything so different?

Because he was different. He missed Jenna. It was as if the sun had gone out of his life. He rubbed his hand over his forehead. He'd waited twelve years, he'd never looked her up when she was in Marietta because he'd been scared. He'd known she was there and it had left him vulnerable. But once she was safely in Alaska, she'd become safe, unavailable. It was pretty damn impossible to be with someone over a thousand miles away.

Once that piece clicked, it was as if the dominoes had all fallen into place. What had Bull Swenson told him? That he'd waited on Merrilee, but finally it was up to her? Jenna had approached him years ago and then she'd waited. She was still waiting and now it was up to him. Now he got the joke and the look that had passed between Merrilee and Bull the evening he'd declared he didn't want to keep Jenna waiting too long. He'd kept her waiting for years. They'd all clearly seen what he'd been too blind to see—that he and Jenna belonged together. He got it…finally. She was independent, definitely her own woman, and she loved him. Equally important, hell, more importantly, he loved her. He finally knew how he felt about her—he loved her madly, passionately, desperately. She made him want to slay dragons and conquer the world, as long as he got to wake up next to her every morning. No, he didn't want her attached at the hip, but he did want her, make that need her, in his life. That much was apparent—even to him, which was saying something. All his life he'd just sort of gone along with what he was supposed to do. Now he needed to decide what he wanted to do. And at the top of that list was figuring out how to make Jenna a part of his life.

There were two options as far as he could tell. Jenna could come here or he could go there. She had made it clear she wasn't coming here. His life was here, which left them with nowhere to go.

He pushed away from his desk and paced from one end of the room to the other, and then back again. Think, Logan, think. His great-grandfather, Jebediah, stared relentlessly at Logan from his portrait on the wall. It was almost as if Logan could hear him speak. "Get outside your comfort zone. Think outside the box. Be bold. Be daring. I didn't discover gold sitting on my duff."

What did Logan really have here? A house that wasn't a home. A family wound so tight, *feelings* was a dirty word. A job he did because it was expected of him. Years of the same.

He thought about how efficient he'd been working in Good Riddance before he'd taken his vacation. He'd done the same damn thing there that he did here—he'd answered emails, reviewed reports, signed off on documents, handled and delegated problems. An idea took root and he began to jot down notes. The internet was alive and well in Good Riddance. He could teleconference and handle his business from there. In actuality, there wasn't a damn thing he did for work in Atlanta that he couldn't do in Good Riddance. True enough, his parents were going to come unglued, not because they'd miss him but because they'd label his behavior as unacceptable.

Did he dare? The real question was did he dare not? Was he going to sit on his ass and do nothing while the best thing that had ever happened to him slipped away from him? Even if Jenna was willing to sit around and wait for him, why would he want to waste any more time?

He began to make a list of what had to be done. Jenna had waited long enough. He was nearly finished when Martina opened her door and poked her head in. "Got a minute?"

"Sure."

Martina came in and sat down across from him. "Okay, look, cuz, we've got to come to an understanding. My friends are about to string me up and run me out of town. I keep fixing you up with them and you keep standing them up. Something's gotta give."

"Yeah, I'm sorry about that."

"You are?" Obviously Martina had expected an argument.

"Yeah, I've put you in sort of a bad spot."

"Are you okay, Logan?" She peered at him. "You just haven't been yourself since you got back from Alaska. Maybe you shouldn't take any more vacations. They seem to screw with your head."

Martina, being the most unorthodox of his very traditional family, seemed the perfect person to talk to about his new life. "I'm getting married. At least I hope I'm getting married." He was pretty sure Jenna wouldn't turn him down when he showed up. Surely she was tired of waiting for him.

Martina shook her head, as if to clear it. "Logan, did you just say you were getting married?"

"I did."

"Don't you have to date someone first?"

"Do you remember Jenna Rathburne from high school?"

"Peppy blonde, big—" she held her hands out in front of her own modest chest "—cheerleader? Yeah, I remember her… Jenna? Get out. I knew you had a thing for her—"

"You did?"

"Well, sure. You're marrying *Jenna?*"

"I certainly hope so. And I'm moving to Alaska."

"You've got some big blanks to fill in for me. And your parents are going to stroke out. They'll think you've lost your mind. Heck, I think you've lost your mind."

More like he'd finally woken up. "My mind's pretty sound but my heart's a goner."

Martina stared at him. "That's it. You've definitely lost your mind." She grinned. "It's about time."

13

LOGAN SAT AT THE round mahogany table in his father's corner office overlooking the Atlanta skyline. His great-grandfather Jebediah Jeffries seemed to be watching him. Only today, it seemed as if Jebediah had a different look in his eye. That unrelenting stare seemed to have softened. Logan could've sworn there was a glint of approval in the old man's eyes.

His father, immaculately turned out in his Brooks Brothers suit, read through a stack of papers. He didn't look up until Martina and Kyle slid into place at the table. Martina mouthed "good luck" to him. Last, but certainly not least, his mother came in and sat next to Martina. His mother wasn't normally part of their business meetings but since this was personal, he figured he'd just go over it the one time. And since his family was all about business, the office seemed the best place to break the news.

Davis Jeffries peered at him over the top of his glasses. "You wanted a meeting?"

Logan nodded. He'd gone over it several times in his head. "I'd like to propose restructuring my position. When I was in Alaska a couple of weeks ago, I realized how much more efficient I was in my job without the in-office interruptions. Therefore, I'd like to begin telecommuting."

Davis frowned. "We've always come into the office every day."

"True. It would be a change, but there are new, more efficient ways of doing business. We have to change with the times or get left behind. I would, of course, come in for the quarterly board meetings."

"You only want to come in quarterly?"

Martina looked steadfastly at her hands folded in her lap. Logan was certain it was to keep from laughing at what she knew was coming.

"Well, the second part of the restructuring involves me relocating."

His mother spoke up. "You want to move? You just redid your condo." She shot Martina a "you're-falling-down-on-your-job" look. "And I thought you were starting to have more of a social life."

"Mother, *you* had my condo remodeled."

"Because there's no other woman in your life to organize that kind of thing." She and his father maintained a very traditional marital division of labor. "Well, where are you thinking of moving? Buckhead? I know it's a little more upscale."

"Alaska."

"Alaska?" His mother looked horrified.

"Alaska?" His father appeared puzzled.

Kyle's mouth simply gaped open.

"Good Riddance to be precise."

"You want to run our business from a remote bush town?" his father said.

"We can give it a shot. If it doesn't work out, I'll tender my resignation."

"Alaska?" His mother was still stuck there.

"And if we don't want to *give it a shot,* as you so cavalierly put it?" Davis managed to inject a wealth of derision in one sentence.

"Then I'll tender my resignation now. I, of course, will cover the position, from Alaska, until you can find a replacement."

His mother had recovered her voice. "Logan Charles Jeffries, why in the world do you want to move to Alaska?" She made it sound synonymous with Hades.

Logan grinned. "Because of a woman, Mother, why else? I'm in love. I'm going to get married if she'll have me."

"Jesus," Kyle breathed.

"No, her name is Jenna," Martina said.

"Davis, do something," his mother said. "Our son needs help. He's lost his mind."

"I'm getting a life."

"Jeffries don't fall in love," his father said.

His mother nodded. "Listen to your father."

His father steepled his fingers in front of his face, a calculating look in his eyes. "Let's not be hasty. What's her family in? Oil? Gas?"

"I'm not sure what her family does, but she does nails."

"Building supplies?" His father nodded slowly. "It's a growing segment."

"No. Nails. Finger nails. Mani/pedis she calls them."

"Dear God."

"Sweet Jesus."

While his father and Kyle invoke a higher power, his mother did one better.

"I feel…faint." And then she collapsed, toppling right over and landing in Martina's lap.

Well, that had gone better than he'd expected.

"You're going to have to tell him, Jenna," Merrilee said as Jenna settled in the chair next to Merrilee's desk at the airstrip office. The sun, in its brief appearance, glimmered through the window.

"I'm going to, Merrilee. I told him I'd let him know. But it seems to me that if he was so worried, he could've picked up the phone and called now, couldn't he? Or, let's see, there's email. Texting. Web-camming. Good old-fashioned letters. But nothing. I haven't heard a word from him."

"Have you ever thought that on his end, he's thinking the same thing? You haven't contacted him.

Communication is a two-way street and you're the one with the big newsflash."

Tears gathered in Jenna's eyes and Merrilee handed her a tissue, patting her hand in the process. "I'm so sick of crying," Jenna said, sniffling. "These hormones are killing me."

She'd never been one to cry, but she'd cried more in the past two weeks than she had in her entire life. And she was tired, all the time. Skye had assured her the tears were all the hormonal changes and in a couple of weeks, she should level out. She hoped so. Between the mood swings and the tears, she could hardly stand herself. No wonder Logan hadn't contacted her. And that made her want to cry all over again.

"Look, hon, go next door and get you and Junior something to eat. Dalton should be landing any minute and then I'll come over and have lunch with you. Go and save me a seat."

Jenna went. As usual, Gus's was packed because Lucky had the soaps running. And Rooster's bookie business had been cranking. Apparently there were a lot of bets as to the baby's sex, weight and if and when the daddy was going to show up.

Sitting at her usual table, Jenna dabbed at her eyes. She hadn't told Logan yet because she wanted him to come back for *her,* not because she was carrying the next Jeffries. She knew he had to walk his own path, she just wished he'd walk it a little faster.

"IT'S ABOUT DAMN TIME," Dalton said without pre-amble.

Logan grinned and shrugged, shaking the other man's hand. "Hey, it takes a little bit of time to turn your life upside down."

"I guess. We'll all be glad to see you. And I'm glad you got here today instead of tomorrow. I just won a hundred bucks."

"Rooster?" The wagers had probably started the day he left town as to how long it would take him to pull his head out of his posterior and make it back.

"Yeah. He's got a quite a few bets going. You are here to stay?"

"If Jenna will have me."

"Well, this should be interesting." Dalton's smile held a sly edge, but that was nothing out of the ordi-nary.

Half an hour later, they rolled to a stop on the air strip. Logan climbed out of the plane before Dalton had killed the engine, eager to be back. He knew ex-actly what Merrilee had meant and how Jenna felt. He'd come home.

He didn't wait for Dalton, crossing to the airstrip in record time. He walked in and Merrilee jumped up. "So, you're the surprise package coming in. Thank goodness. It's about time." She hugged him. His own mother hadn't even hugged him when he left. But then again, she was pretty disappointed in his decisions, and that was putting it lightly. "I was afraid we were going to have to kidnap you and drag you back."

"Where is she?"

Merrilee nodded toward the connecting door. "Gus's."

He was halfway across the room.

"Logan…" He looked back over his shoulder. "She's missed you."

"That's good to know. I've missed her, too."

"Welcome home."

Yeah, yeah. He wanted Jenna. Nodding, he pushed open the door to Gus's.

"Well…"

"It's about time."

"Holy smokes."

"He's back."

"Someone hand me the remote."

"But this is a good part."

"Hit the Mute. This is gonna be even better."

The televisions and the whole room went quiet. Kind of like the first night he was here and wanted to walk her home. He didn't mind providing the entertainment, as long as he got what he wanted. And what he wanted was Jenna.

He looked to the table in the back right corner, his gaze tangling with hers.

"Hi," he said.

"Hi. You came back."

"Yeah. I left something important."

"Merrilee could've shipped it for you."

She wasn't going to make it easy. "Nah. It doesn't work that way."

"Why are you here this time?"

"For the same reason I came the first time."

"Logan, you don't get it. The town's not for sale."

"*You* don't get it, Jenna. I came for you." He reached into his pocket and pulled out a jeweler's box. "I love you, Jenna." He hesitated. "I don't know your middle name—"

"Louisa."

"I love you, Jenna Louisa Rathburne, and I'd be the happiest man alive if you'd do me the honor of becoming my wife." How was that for getting in touch with his feelings?

She glared at him. "Did someone call you? Who called you?"

What the hell? He was standing here like an idiot. This wasn't turning out at all like he'd planned. But then again, his plans seemed to go awry when they involved Jenna. "You don't want to marry me?"

She pushed to her feet, her eyes swimming with tears. "I wouldn't marry you if you were the last man on earth." She marched to the door. He started after her.

"Don't you dare follow me, you stalker."

"You said it'd be romantic if I flew all this way for you, not stalkerish. Make up your mind. Besides, what happened to *I love you, Logan?*"

"That was before."

Dammit. He was confused and he didn't like being

confused. "Before? Before what? Before I actually turned everything upside down to come back to be with you?"

She walked out the front door of Gus's.

There was a chorus of "Follow her" all around him.

Merrilee gave him a gentle push from behind. "It's going to be okay. Go get her."

Logan caught up with Jenna before she reached the door to the Bed & Breakfast. Everybody streamed out of Gus's behind him.

He caught her arm, turning her to face him. "What's going on, Jenna? Sometimes I have a hard time following your logic but this time, I'm really missing an important piece of the puzzle. Help me out, honey."

She shook off his hand. "This is humiliating. Everybody knows why you're here."

"Sure they do. Because I just told you I loved you in front of damn near everyone. And then I proposed." He'd never seen her cry before. Her blue eyes were brimming.

"But I want you to want to marry me because you want to, not because of the baby."

"I almost followed that... Wait. Did you say baby?" He felt sort of dizzy. Had he heard... "Baby?" He looked over his shoulder. "Did she say baby?"

"Uh-huh," Merrilee said, nodding.

He turned back to Jenna. "Baby? We're going to have a baby?"

"You didn't know?"

"We're, you and I..." He made a rocking motion with his arms. "Us...for real?"

"You didn't know." This was a statement rather than a question. A hint of her sunny smile curved her lips. "You really didn't know about the baby." Her smile blossomed. "You want to marry me because you want to marry me."

Laughing she flung herself into his arms and kissed him like he'd never been kissed before. She wrapped her arms around his neck and leaned back. "Yes, Logan, we're going to have a baby."

Joy like he'd never known before filled him. He picked her up and whirled her around. Holding her tight, he grinned at his new neighbors and announced, "We're going to have a baby."

Merrilee beamed at him. "On behalf of everyone here, welcome to Good Riddance, where you get to leave behind what ails you."

* * * * *

COMING NEXT MONTH

Available October 25, 2011

#645 THE SURVIVOR
Men Out of Uniform
Rhonda Nelson

#646 MODEL MARINE
Uniformly Hot!
Candace Havens

#647 THE MIGHTY QUINNS: DANNY
The Mighty Quinns
Kate Hoffmann

#648 INTOXICATING
Lori Wilde

#649 ROPED IN
The Wrong Bed
Crystal Green

#650 ROYALLY CLAIMED
A Real Prince
Marie Donovan

HBCNM1011

REQUEST YOUR FREE BOOKS!
2 FREE NOVELS PLUS 2 FREE GIFTS!

Harlequin *Blaze*

red-hot reads!

Harlequin® Special Edition® is thrilled to present a new installment in USA TODAY bestselling author RaeAnne Thayne's reader-favorite miniseries,
THE COWBOYS OF COLD CREEK.

Join the excitement as we meet the Bowmans—four siblings who lost their parents but keep family ties alive in Pine Gulch. First up is Trace. Only two things get under this rugged lawman's skin: beautiful women and secrets. And in Rebecca Parsons, he finds both!

Read on for a sneak peek of
CHRISTMAS IN COLD CREEK.
Available November 2011 from Harlequin® Special Edition®.

On impulse, he unfolded himself from the bar stool. "Need a hand?"

"Thank you! I…" She lifted her gaze from the floor to his jeans and then raised her eyes. When she identified him her hazel eyes turned from grateful to unfriendly and cold, as if he'd somehow thrown the broken glasses at her head.

He also thought he saw a glimmer of panic in those interesting depths, which instantly stirred his curiosity like cream swirling through coffee.

"I've got it, Officer. Thank you." Her voice was several degrees colder than the whirl of sleet outside the windows.

Despite her protests, he knelt down beside her and began to pick up shards of broken glass. "No problem. Those trays can be slippery."

This close, he picked up the scent of her, something fresh and flowery that made him think of a mountain meadow on a July afternoon. She had a soft, lush mouth and for one brief, insane moment, he wanted to push aside that stray lock of hair slipping from her ponytail and taste her. Apparently he needed to spend a lot less time working and a great deal *more* time recreating with the opposite sex if he could have sudden random fantasies about a woman he wasn't even inclined to like, pretty or not.

"I'm Trace Bowman. You must be new in town."

She didn't answer immediately and he could almost see the wheels turning in her head. Why the hesitancy? And why that little hint of unease he could see clouding the edge of her gaze? His presence was obviously making her uncomfortable and Trace couldn't help wondering why.

"Yes. We've been here a few weeks."

"Well, I'm just up the road about four lots, in the white house with the cedar shake roof, if you or your daughter need anything." He smiled at her as he picked up the last shard of glass and set it on her tray.

Definitely a story there, he thought as she hurried away. He just might need to dig a little into her background to find out why someone with fine clothes and nice jewelry, and who so obviously didn't have experience as a waitress, would be here slinging hash at The Gulch. Was she running away from someone? A bad marriage?

So...Rebecca Parsons. Not Becky. An intriguing woman. It had been a long time since one of those had crossed his path here in Pine Gulch.

Trace won't rest until he finds out Rebecca's secret, but will he still have that same attraction to her once he does? Find out in CHRISTMAS IN COLD CREEK. Available November 2011 from Harlequin® Special Edition®.

Discover two classic tales of romance in one
incredible volume from

USA TODAY Bestselling Author

Catherine Mann

Two powerful, passionate men
are determined to win back the women
who haunt their dreams...but it will
take more than just seduction
to convince them that this love will last.

IRRESISTIBLY HIS

Available October 25, 2011.

Harlequin® *Desire*

ALWAYS POWERFUL. PASSIONATE AND PROVOCATIVE.

NEW YORK TIMES AND **USA TODAY**
BESTSELLING AUTHOR

BRENDA JACKSON

**PRESENTS A BRAND-NEW TALE
OF SEDUCTION**

TEMPTATION

TEXAS CATTLEMAN'S CLUB: THE SHOWDOWN

Millionaire security expert and rancher Zeke Travers
always separates emotion from work. Until a case
leads him to Sheila Hopkins—and the immediate,
scorching heat that leaped between them. Suddenly,
Zeke is tempted to break the rules. And it's only a
matter of time before he gives in....

Available November wherever books are sold.